AWAKENED

Published by

Two Realms Publishing LLC

**https://tworealmspublishingllc.com**

Book Cover by We Got You Covered Book Design

Illustrations by Nicodemus Holroyd

ISBN: 978-1-955106-22-1

Printed in the United States of America

# AWAKENED

## The Guardhian Series

## Book One

## Krys Fenner

# DEDICATION

One choice makes all the difference in the world.

**Niamh:** pronounced Nee-iv

**Quinlan**: pronounced kwin-lynn

**Jarrett**: pronounced jer-et

**Súil na Éireannach**: Eyes of the Irish

**Bygleswurth**: pronounced big-uls-wurth

**Meara**: pronounced Me-r-ah

**Dava**: pronounced Day-vah

**Guardhian**: a person/creature with power used for guarding one of nine realms created by the gods

**Catalync**: pronounced cat-ah-link; lynx-like creature with blue-gray fur and spiked tail that serves as a guide to Guardhians

**Prohtector**: a person/creature who aids and protects Guardhians

**Dia dhuit ar 'maidin**: good morning

**I bhfad ar shiúl**: far away

**An Talamh Beo**: The Living Land

**Grianne**: pronounced gree-on

**Ainsley**: pronounced ain-zlee

**Nessan**: pronounced nah-sawn

**Grullac**: pronounced gru-loc; olive-green creature with long claws serving as warriors under dark god Ci'Haran

**Trekasha**: pronounced tray-ka-shuh; tree-spirit that serves under goddess Di'Lacia and may be called upon for help

**Solfhionn**: pronounced sul-fee-awn; white phoenix; humanoid creature, under goddess Di'Lacia, with pointed ears, white wings, pure heart and soul that typically lives between five hundred and six hundred years

**Di'Lacia**: pronounced die-lay-sea-ah; goddess over the realm of An Talamh Beo; daughter of the goddess Dana; member of Tuatha de Danann

**Feid'Helm**: pronounced fide-helm; god who fell in love with the goddess Di'Lacia

**Ci'Haran**: pronounced sy-hare-in; dark god who also fell in love with the goddess Di'Lacia

**Normal**: non-magical person/creature

**Trainhor**: humanoid/creature responsible for teaching Guardhians how to use their powers and fight

**Rhea**: pronounced Ray-ah

# CHAPTER ONE

THE HOWLING WIND PIERCED *Niamh's ears as she lay sprawled out on the ground. Her fire-red hair whipped all around her face. As she snapped back into consciousness, she groaned and slowly rolled to her side. She reached up to the corner of her mouth and wiped at the blood trickling down her chin and then lifted her gaze to the noise only ten feet away. She blinked at the sight before her.*

*Near to where she laid, two men battled one another. Neither of her blades could cut the aggression given off by the two of them. To make matters worse, her brother appeared to be winning.*

*A dark flare shone brightly in his once green eyes as his opponent's blade pierced just beneath his collarbone on the right side. He laughed ¼ with no gusto, no heart. There was nothing that reflected amusement in his laugh. It was closer to the cackle of a hyena than anything else. Blood soaked through his clean white pressed cotton shirt. In a gruff voice, he yelled, "Is that the best ye can do?"*

*Her brother's fist connected with his opponent's broad chin. Despite their height and weight difference, the tank of a guy, Jarrett, stumbled back a few steps and his sienna brown hair fell out of place.*

*There had to be something she could do. She had power. She knew how to wield it. This was the fight that would alter her future forever. Getting to her feet, Niamh focused on collecting a shockwave in her hands. She had to time the release perfectly; otherwise, she chanced harming the wrong person.*

*Her brother's lips curled fiercely into a deep grin as he yanked the blade from his shoulder. No sound escaped his mouth. A breath of air could hardly be noticed as he removed the twelve-inch, double-edged dagger from his body. It seemed to cause him no pain, or perhaps he merely reveled in it. Taking advantage of the tank's stumbling, he stepped forward with a full grip on the hilt of the blade and swiped at him.*

*Jarrett jerked his face back and barely avoided getting cut with his own blade. The swipe missed by less than an inch.*

*Her brother was shorter than the tank. He found the momentum needed to gather his footing and spun around, striking her brother with an elbow jab to the throat.*

*She needed more time. This shockwave had to be the most powerful she had ever dispersed. Niamh watched on as the fight progressed and continued to focus the gathering ball of energy through her entire body.*

*Her brother used the force of the tank's steps and shoved the double-edged dagger with full strength into the back of his shoulder. He cackled with glee as his opponent cried out from the pain. "Come on! Ye were s'posed to be this high an' mighty warrior! I thought this would be a challenge!"*

*Backing away, a wrinkle settled upon the bridge of his nose and beads of sweat formed on his brow. Gritting his teeth, he placed his hand on the hilt and yanked the blade from his shoulder. He threw his head back and howled, then faltered and fell to his knees.*

*Niamh screamed.*

*He couldn't die! The agony in his outcry provided her the strength to charge the strongest force of shockwave she'd ever managed. A blue current crackled all over her body. Her normal emerald green irises changed to a deep aqua blue.*

*She was ready.*

*It was time to end this.*

*Her brother's eyes twitched. With a Cheshire grin, he planted his feet firmly against the ground. He shook his arms out, then went completely rigid. His eyes were the same shade of green as hers. At least they had been. Midnight black replaced the once emerald green that filled his eyes.*

*Niamh unleashed the full weight of the shockwave that had consumed her entire body. Blue electricity shot out from her arms, her legs, her fingers. The shockwave surged from every part of her toward her brother.*

*The energy pushed him back and tore at his skin, but it didn't knock him down. Hardly any skin ripped open. Wait ... no, it was healing, repairing itself before her very eyes! It hadn't been strong enough. It hadn't been the right call. The right power. The one she needed to defeat him once and for all.*

*Her brother lunged at her and wrapped his gangly hand tightly around her neck. Lifting her off the ground, he grinned. "See, I was just goin' to kill ye, but now I get to kill both o'ye."*

*The air in her lungs constricted.*

*"Ye...don't...wan...to...do...this," she mustered out between tiny breaths.*

*Tightening his hold around her neck, he pulled her face closer to his. He locked his gaze with her green eyes. "Súil na Éireannach."*

*The grin on his lips broadened as his other hand reached out and stroked her sultry red hair. His grip tightened again. Color drained from her face as she struggled to breathe.*

*This wasn't how it was supposed to end.*

*She was the one who was supposed to be victorious.*

*She was supposed to save them all.*

*"Killin' ye first an' making 'em watch will be my pleasure."*

*Slowly Jarrett stood. Jumping into action, he ran toward them like a bull charging its handler. "Niamh!"*

Abruptly, Niamh sat up, gasping for air. Wiping the beads of sweat from her brow, she looked around. She half expected to find her brother hovering over her with his hands wrapped tightly around her neck. That wasn't the case.

She was at home, in her bedroom. There was no movement from the Horslips or the Phil Lynott posters that hung on the wall. Both her dresser and desk were completely still. She heard the wind bustling against her bedroom window. There was no movement from her closet; her clothes hung just as she had left them.

Inhaling deeply, the pounding of her heart finally slowed. She eyed the clock on her nightstand. It was just barely three in the morning. She glanced down at the end of her bed where her cat's head had popped up the instant she moved. "C'mere, Bygleswurth."

He meowed at her softly as he stretched up to his full size. His blue-gray fur shimmered in the stream of moonlight coming through her window. His entire body jiggled as he paraded toward her. He was no small cat, weighing close to twenty pounds. Most of it was fat, though she described him as comfortably plump. Still, the one thing that stood out the most was the small patch of white fur on his chin, which to her hinted at a beard.

Niamh tugged him into her lap and ruffled his fur. She giggled at the way his maw pursed. "Sorry. I know ye don't like that. I wish ye could talk. Then maybe you could explain these nightmares I have about me brother."

"Meeeeeeeoo ... details ... ooowwww."

What in the world? Had there been a word mixed in there? Impossible. This was a cat. Raising an eyebrow, she laughed at herself. She probably imagined the whole thing. "Bygleswurth, I swear ye just talked to me."

Shaking the outlandish idea out of her head, she allowed Bygleswurth to nestle in her lap. She'd had this dream before. She reached over to her nightstand, opened a drawer, and carefully withdrew her journal. She'd kept track of the nightmares since they began. It always seemed to be the same one. Frequently, she had tried to peer deeper into the nightmare, hoping for some clue on what it meant. All she'd been able to decipher was that her brother appeared to relish the idea of killing her.

Besides, there were still a few other things in the dream she didn't understand. Who was the man defending her? What had she been summoning? And where was all of it taking place? None of it made any sense, which was exactly why she recorded them.

She jotted down everything she recalled about the dream and returned the journal to her nightstand. A chill passed through the room and Niamh shuddered. It was just a nightmare, not something that would ever come to pass.

Gently, she hefted Bygleswurth from her lap and pulled the covers back. She climbed out of bed and tiptoed to her bedroom door. Cracking the door open, she poked her head out to make sure nobody noticed her waking up. The hallway was completely empty. She slipped out of her room and headed down the hall. Sneaking past her brother's room, she paused for a minute when the floorboard creaked, then continued on her way down the stairs.

Their house had been in the family for an entire century. She was only five when her parents told her that. Since then, she'd climbed and crawled through every nook and hole she could find. At one point, she'd gone to the library to conduct some research on their home. She was certain the house held some secrets, but all she'd ever discovered was that her great grandfather built the house in 1872. One time she was positive she could prove the house was haunted, but it turned out to be a family of mice. Six months ago, the faint pitter-pattering stopped. She suspected her brother had something to do with it.

She lingered on the bottom step of the staircase. Three distinct voices came from the kitchen. At least two belonged to her parents, but she couldn't identify the third. All of which was highly unusual. At this time of hour, everyone was normally asleep. Explained why neither her mother nor father checked on her. Chewing on the inside of her cheek, she glanced from the kitchen door to the hallway on her left. She had two options: go listen at the kitchen door, or continue in her original direction to the parlor, her go-to after a nightmare.

Feck.

Niamh glided through the dining room and crept to the connecting kitchen door. It hadn't been shut all the way. She peeked through the crack and spotted her mother at the table and some tall, dark-headed man hovering nearby. He didn't look familiar, but that didn't mean he wasn't associated with the men she'd seen come in and out of her father's pub. Where was her father? She had a limited view from this angle, but it would really be nice to see what he was doing.

"Why don't ye head upstairs, my love, while I finish up 'ere?" her father said.

A red light pulsated behind the dark-haired man. He put his hand on her mother's shoulder and squeezed. "I don't think she'll be going anywhere. I told you, Quinlan. Don't make it any harder than it has to be."

*What the hell is that?* The light didn't appear to be coming from outside. It actually seemed as if it emanated from the man. Was he a shifter? No, couldn't be. She'd seen her brother transition into his wolf form, and that never happened. Niamh rubbed her eyes and peered back through the slit between the door and the doorjamb. The light was gone.

"Leave her out of this, Rooney," her father snapped

"Tomorrow morning, Quinlan. I'll stop by the pub first thing. Have Séamus's cut ready...or else." He released his grip on her mother's shoulder and headed for the back door. "Don't make me wait."

Rooney exited, slamming the door shut behind him.

Her mother shot up from the table and her father raced from the corner of the kitchen. The two met in the middle and embraced.

Frowning, Niamh slunk back through the dining room and upstairs to her bedroom. What in the world was that about? She knew her father dealt with some shady men, but she'd witnessed none of his dealings firsthand. She always thought it was small time stuff, like obtaining some illegal liquor or something, but nothing like this. Not to mention the weird light that came from that man. What could that have been?

She slid into her bedroom and closed the door. Leaning against it, she ran her fingers through her red hair. Her dream. In it, she had practically glowed and shot a blue light from her hands. Was it linked to the light she saw coming from the man?

That didn't make any sense. None of this made any sense. She knew one thing for sure.

Something bad was coming.

And it was darker than the night sky.

Quinlan rolled over and eyeballed the digital clock on his nightstand. Six-thirty in the morning. It was way too early to be up. He'd barely slept three hours, not that he didn't shoot for more, but he was restless. The hamster wheel in his head refused to settle. All he could think about was everything he had to teach his daughter and how little time he had to do it.

His world was slowly collapsing around him and there wasn't much he could do to stop it. This was both good and bad. He dragged a hand down his face. He couldn't pretend any longer it wasn't happening.

The shift in his daughter had already begun. He'd sensed the static as he and his wife walked by Niamh's bedroom earlier. Her powers were awakening. He wasn't surprised. She had just turned thirteen, and every Guardhian gained their sight at that age.

It was how it always started.

He just wasn't ready. He hadn't taught his daughter about her heritage the way his cousin Ainsley had taught her son, Nessan. At least he could say Nessan would make a good Prohtector for Niamh. One small benefit of Ainsley raising him the way she had.

He should've followed suit, then they wouldn't be in this position; though it may not have made a difference.

Quinlan sighed. Either way, he couldn't change it now. He eased his arm from beneath his wife, climbed out of bed, and threw on a pair of jeans and a t-shirt. He'd grab his boots a little later. At that moment, he needed to delay his meeting. He had much more important things to accomplish first.

He headed downstairs to his office. Sitting down at his desk, he glanced from the picture-frame to the left of the calendar, then to the right. The one on the left was of his family. His wife, Dava, his daughter, Niamh, holding that damn catalync, him and his son, Quinlan Jr. He picked up the frame on the right. It was of him, Dava, and Meara. All three of them were light-skinned, not that it made them look alike. His and Dava's red hair contrasted with Meara's long, midnight black locks.

Meara was the one who was supposed to teach Niamh about her powers and her responsibility to the realm. But the woman had disappeared three years ago. No one in his immediate circle had figured out where she'd gone off; which meant the responsibility fell on him. He didn't have a clue how that would work.

He couldn't think about that right then, not with everything else on his mind. Quinlan set the frame back down, lifted the phone from the receiver and dialed his boss.

The line rang twice, and Séamus answered. "Good morning, Quinlan. To what do I owe this pleasure?"

Part of him had truly hoped the guy wouldn't answer, except it wouldn't have resolved anything. And he couldn't have that. He rubbed his thumb above his brow. He had to be smart about how he addressed his issue. "I called 'bout the visit I received last night from Rooney."

"Oh? I cannot imagine he was unclear regarding what I am due."

Quinlan swallowed and bit his tongue. Every inch of him wanted to punch Séamus in his fat, rosy-cheeked face, but it would get him nothing save for a beat-down. Even if it made him feel better, it would be temporary. He could handle this, as long as he kept his cool. "Nothing's overdue. Ye know how long it takes. Didn't anybody ever teach you patience is a virtue?"

Sarcasm wasn't the wisest decision, but a bullet through the phone was physically impossible. He'd live to see another day. Besides, there wasn't anyone to take his place ... yet.

"Just because me mother taught me manners does not mean ye can use that to get out of this. My cut is late! It is that simple. So you best have it ready when Rooney comes."

"I'm going to have it. I just need 'til tonight."

He had the money in his safe at the pub. It was all set and ready to go, but he needed time with his daughter. He had to take her to the cabin—*today*. He'd put it off too long, and she had a lot to learn.

"All right, Quinlan. I will give you 'til tonight." Séamus paused and went quiet for a couple of beats. "But only if your lil' girl is there when it is collected."

His daughter? Why would his boss stipulate Niamh had to be there? What was his game? It made no sense. Not to mention he sure as hell didn't want to do it. He swore he would never get Niamh involved in his business. Yeah, she helped at the pub, but nothing with that side of the business. It was bad enough his wife had gotten entangled in that part of his life, but she was wicked good with numbers.

What other choice did he have? Séamus had a vice grip on him and the guy knew it. Not that it should be a big deal. Niamh had been around a few times when Rooney had swung by the pub. Tonight would be no different. Quinlan nodded. "Agreed."

"Excellent. I look forward to meeting 'er." The phone line went dead.

His eyes widened and sweat bloomed on the inside of his palm. The sound of silence from the phone didn't last. It soon turned into sharp, loud beeps. Quinlan stared at the receiver.

What the hell had he just done?

# CHAPTER TWO

"Niamh," a voice whispered. She swatted at her ear. She had to be hearing things. It was too early in the morning for anyone in her family to be up.

"Niamh," her father called again.

Her eyes slowly fluttered open. Light streamed in from the doorway, but nowhere else. It was still dark outside her window. She glanced over her shoulder at the figure looming in her bedroom door. That was her father standing there? Right? It was hard to tell through the black discoloration surrounding the person's outline.

"*Daidí?*"

Stepping inside, he kneeled down next to her bed and smiled. The shadow disappeared. Everything appeared normal: from his scruffy beard to the strawberry color of his red hair to the green eyes they all shared. *"Dia dhuit ar 'maidin."*

*"Dia dhuit ar 'maidin."* Bidding him good morning, Niamh rolled over onto her back and quirked an eyebrow. He was flashing her one of those sorrowful smiles he wore sometimes. Like whatever was about to happen was both happy and sad at the same time. She'd noticed them more in the last few weeks. Come to think of it, he'd sported them a lot since her thirteenth birthday.

Either way, it was weird and not her father's normal weird. He'd always treated her differently than her brother. She was the precious gem, similar to everyone else, but completely unique. At least, that was how her father described her. Which was why it was strange her father sat there in her room on a Saturday morning. So what if it was—her eyes skimmed over the clock on her nightstand—nearly seven in the morning. Her father spent Saturday with her brother, not her.

"Is everything all right, Daidí?"

"Yes. We have some errands to run this morning."

"We do?" Niamh sat up in bed and brushed her hair out of her face. He hadn't mentioned anything before about this. What was going on? First, his secret meeting the night before with that strange, angry man, and now this. She studied her father's electric green eyes to see if she could find out what was happening.

Over the years, she and her father had developed their own silent language. His eyes had always been the key. His gaze lowered toward the wooden floor.

Nothing. She couldn't see anything beyond the eye color they shared. Whatever he had planned, he kept it well hidden. His eyes were completely unreadable. For once, she wished she'd learned more about *Súil na aÉireannach,* or Eyes of the Irish. Maybe then she'd comprehend whatever was going on behind her father's hooded eyes.

"That's because it was something I decided last minute. Now, come on and get dressed, but be quiet. We don't want to wake your brother and mother." He stood.

It wasn't unusual for the two of them to go off and do something together without the rest of their family. But why did it matter if they were awake? Her father had never cared before. How many times had she gone into her brother's bedroom with a bucket of water when he wouldn't wake up? Too many to count. And it was always to get him moving; whether she and her father were heading off or they all were leaving. Niamh opened her mouth—

"Ah, stall the ball. We need to get goin'. Okay? I promise I'll answer your questions on the road."

Niamh crossed her arms and her lips tightened. She didn't enjoy waiting for answers. By the time she'd get any, she'd have a million more. One question always led to two, which led to four, and eventually led to twenty or more questions.

"Mrrooo ... tell ... ooooowwww."

Eyeballing Bygleswurth, she scratched at her ear. She really needed to get her hearing checked. Maybe whatever her father intended for them to do together could involve a visit to the doctor. Either that or she was losing her mind.

Her father grinned. "Ye should bring Bygleswurth along. I'm sure he wouldn't mind gettin' outta the house."

"Mmmmrrrrrrooooo ... mad ... oowww. Mmmrr ... out ... oooooooowwww."

Maybe she didn't speak cat, but that was the clearest and loudest protest she'd ever heard, though she could've sworn she actually heard human words come out of his maw. Nah. Bygleswurth was a cat and cats didn't speak. Yeah. She was definitely hearing things. It was probably because of the lack of sleep. It had been late when she'd gone back to bed after her nightmare.

"I'll see ye both downstairs." Her father left her bedroom.

Bygleswurth stretched, jumped down from the bed, and pranced toward the door. He meowed again loudly as the door shut in his face. He flicked his tail in the air and turned around.

Niamh giggled and climbed out of bed. That had been the funniest thing to watch. It almost appeared that her cat chased after her father. But that was ridiculous. She scooped up Bygleswurth. "Gettin' out of the house won't be so bad. Besides, you like car rides."

"Mmmmeee ... will not travel ... ooowwww. Mmm ... will be ... ee ... physically exhausting ... ooowww." Bygleswurth snorted.

She shook her head and set him back on the ground. Maybe a day away from the house would be good for her, too. She could use some air to clear her head and ears, because she was definitely hearing something. If only she knew what. She strode across her bedroom to her dresser, snagged her hairbrush, and pulled her hair into a ponytail. With one task complete, she pulled out drawers and got dressed.

Nessan turned down a country road, throwing up a plume of dust in his truck's wake. He glimpsed cattle grazing not far off from the barbed wire fencing as he drove toward the pack house. Normally, he wouldn't be about this early in the morning, but the alpha had summoned him. Though he didn't have any clue what it regarded. At least he didn't think it had to do with their conversation a few days ago. He'd given his cousin the message. Not that Quinlan had been all that receptive.

The stench of cow manure assaulted his nostrils. With a groan, he wiggled his nose. Yeah, because that would cover the smell of wolf. It was a good thing only other shape shifters knew about this place. Otherwise, people might question the existence of an animal believed extinct for nearly two centuries. He shook his head as he slowed his truck and hooked a left, passing an old rotting shack. It served as a deterrent to outsiders and a marker for everyone else.

He followed the indistinct path of the dirt road, winding around beyond the gates, and by the guards, until the sprawling farmhouse came into view. Nessan slowed his speed as several pack members strolled across the land toward various parts of the ranch. Everyone who lived here contributed. He wasn't a full-fledged member because of his duties to the realm's guardhian. As one of three bear shapeshifters in at least the county, it worked out in his favor.

Parking his truck next to the litany of other vehicles there, he shut off the ignition and headed toward the porch. He ascended the short staircase, walked by the empty rocking chairs, and knocked on the door. As one who didn't live here, he'd never just walked into the house, though the alpha and luna had given him permission for it. His mother raised him to have respect.

The door opened.

"Luna Teamhair," Nessan said as he bowed his head. "I hope ye doin' well."

"Grand. C'mon in. Fionn's waitin' for ye." She stepped aside, giving him more than enough room to enter the house.

Wolves and their jokes. He didn't take up that much space. With a faint smirk, Nessan strode into the house. "Do ye know what he needed to see me for?"

"Luna," a pretty brunette hollered as she exited the dining room. "The oven's banjaxed again."

"Have Liam look at it. I'm sure he can fix it," Teamhair replied. "I'll be down in a minute to get breakfast on the table." She swept her hand toward the staircase as her gaze flicked back to him. "Let's go."

Nessan dipped his chin and followed her. As they walked, he glanced over his shoulder at the brunette. She disappeared into the dining room, muttering under her breath. He hadn't seen her here before, not that he interacted with the other shapeshifters much. His duty to Niamh required he remained single until she reached her full power. Only then could he take a mate.

"Don't even think about it," Teamhair said, snapping her fingers in his face. "She's only just got here and needs more stability than ye can offer."

"I don't know what you're talkin' about." The demands of his position weren't a secret, especially from the luna. She knew just as the alpha did what limitations applied to him. Nessan focused his attention forward as they headed to the second floor. "Ye didn't answer my question."

"He wants to talk to you about it himself."

That didn't sound good. Two meetings in one week was already ominous enough, but compounded with what the luna couldn't say—it bothered him a lot. It couldn't have anything to do with the realm. He'd traveled there yesterday and checked in with Grianne. According to the solfhionn, nothing out of the ordinary had happened. All was quiet.

They made their way to the alpha's office around the corner. Teamhair opened the door and Nessan strode in after her. He stopped and bowed his head to the dark-haired male. "Alpha Fionn."

The male stood, rising to his full height of six-foot, five-inches, and strode over to the luna. He leaned down, brushed a kiss across her lips, and let out a deep rumble. "Thank ye for escortin' him up. I s'pose this means you're stayin'."

"I have to get breakfast on the table. The stove's gone wonky again on me. Besides, ye don't need me here."

Fionn tilted his head. "I'll always need ye, but I won't interfere with breakfast."

The pack would have his head without food. Thank the gods he didn't have to spend a bunch of time around here. Seeing this all the time would drive him insane. He didn't move as the alpha and luna exchanged one more kiss before she left, closing the door behind her.

"Have a seat," Fionn stated as he gestured to a nearby chair and returned to his own seat.

Nessan followed the male's instruction. "I'm sure you're wonderin' about Quinlan. I have spoken with him regarding Niamh's training. I'm certain her powers will awaken any day now and he'll have no choice on the matter." It was a bit of an assumption, but it was the only thing that made sense.

"Ah, sound. But that's not why I called ye here."

"Oh?" He raised an eyebrow. He'd jumped to the conclusion, but it had repercussions that explained Teamhair's earlier response. What else could they need him for?

"We've had reports of humans being attacked in Barna Woods. I sent two of my best hunters to investigate. Only one returned. What he's sayin' … he's in bits. I can't think of any other way to describe it."

"Just from a trip to Barna Woods?" It didn't make any sense. That was a tourist destination. A place where humans interacted freely with nature. Surely, he would've heard about any problems.

Fionn nodded. "I think ye should see him for yourself."

"I can do that, but is that why ye called me here?" He highly doubted it. There was more than what the alpha had shared with him.

"I want ye to check it out. I believe this falls under the guardhian's responsibilities, but given our conversation a few days ago, I sent my men instead." The male retrieved a file from a desk drawer and held it out to Nessan. "Go ahead. Look."

Nessan accepted the file, flipped it open, and skimmed through several human reports. Each of which mentioned a dark figure unlike anything they'd ever seen before. It had no face, no voice, no body. Fionn was right. This was something Niamh should investigate; except she didn't even know the truth yet. Nor had her powers awakened. Even if they would soon, she had no training. He sighed. "I'll look into this. Let me talk to the shifter first."

"Very good. I need answers quickly." The male stood. "This can't continue."

"Agreed." Nessan got to his feet. But it was his job to protect Niamh. He could do that while Quinlan figured things out. The alpha led him out of the office and down two flights of stairs. Based on what Fionn had originally said, he thought they'd go to the medical facility, but that wasn't the case. They went to the prison beneath the house.

Nessan stared at the shapeshifter inside the prison cell. Although words came out of the male's mouth, it wasn't any language he'd ever heard before. He glanced at Fionn. "Do ye know what he's sayin'?"

"I hoped you would."

"Shit," he muttered. How did the male even make it back to the ranch in this condition? What had caused it? Was there a cure? Or was the male stuck like this? Several questions and he had to find the answers. "I'll 'andle this. Don't send anyone else."

"Thank ye," Fionn replied.

Niamh stared out the passenger side window and eyed the never-ending sea of green. There were so many deep colors, she could barely tell where one ended and another began. They'd driven for nearly two hours. It wasn't the first time she'd traveled outside Kinvara with her family, but she couldn't remember the last time she'd seen so much lush landscape.

Her father slowed the truck down for a side road she hardly noticed. She imagined if one didn't know about it, they could easily pass the dirt road. Niamh watched as her father drove on for about a mile and then pulled off into a small alcove. It was a space cut into limestone.

She tucked a loose wisp of hair behind her ear and eyed the alcove. How was this even possible? Forest, not a cliff or anything like it surrounded them. Yet she surely stared at what appeared to be the outer part of a cave. And her father's truck fit into it perfectly.

"It's okay, sweetheart. We pick up by foot from here."

"By foot to where? I don't see any proper direction for us to go."

Her father had given her nothing during the car ride. Her cat hadn't even piped up. It had been utterly quiet. No matter what she asked of her father or how many ways she posed the same question, he hadn't told her anything about their so-called plans for the day. He could take her to Blarney for all she knew. Not that they were anywhere near ... well, any town. Why did it feel like her father had taken her to where her brother probably stretched his legs in his wolf form?

"We're heading to the Aillwee Caves."

"The Aillwee Caves?! Then why'd we drive around for the last couple of hours?" It made absolutely no sense. The caves were only about a half-hour from their town. Why would they have taken the longest route possible to get there? Not to mention they weren't near any part of the caves she'd toured before.

"Mmmeee ... goodness sakes, tell her ... ooowww."

Her father glared at Bygleswurth. "You're not helpin' any with this."

"Mmmee ... job ... eeee ... simply to help her."

It was official. They had both gone mad. Perhaps that man from last night had put something in the air or in their water or cast a spell. That would explain the weird light she'd seen emanating from him. It made perfect sense, but she hadn't a clue how to resolve the issue.

"Then help her by helpin' me explain this to her," her father said.

Bygleswurth turned around and climbed up into her lap with his two front paws. "What the old man is attempting to tell you ... mmmeee ... dear, is that you are special."

Frozen in place, she gawked at the *cat* with wide eyes. It was a frigging cat! And she just heard it. That didn't happen. She didn't hear words come out of its maw. It was a cat. And cats didn't talk. She had to be dreaming. That was it. She'd fallen asleep on the roof beneath the stars. Niamh pinched her arm. "Ow."

"What are ye doin'?" her father asked.

She smacked herself across the cheek. It wasn't working. Why wasn't it working? Her heart thudded loudly in her ears. "Tryin' to wake up! Because I have to be dreamin'. Cats don't talk."

"I am no cat. I am a catalync and I prefer you refer to me as such." Bygleswurth harrumphed and flicked his tail.

"Hey, now. Be careful with that thing." Her father leaned back against the driver's side door and regarded her. "Niamh, listen to me. You're not dreamin'. I promise this is all real. If ye don't believe me, look at Bygleswurth again. Really look at 'em. Does he look like a cat to ye?"

*Not dreaming. I'm not dreaming,* she thought to herself. Swallowing saliva to wet her parched throat, she did as her father instructed and focused her attention on Bygleswurth. The creature she had known for years shifted before her eyes.

He grew in size. Although he was still plump, he was more proportionate and quite larger than a normal house cat. His ears elongated. Small wisps stuck out from the tip of each ear. The biggest change was his tail. It was no longer blue-gray, but darker and covered in spikes with a hook at the end.

What the feck? Niamh jumped back, but she couldn't go far. There was a door in her way. She yanked on the seatbelt. Why wouldn't it unbuckle?

Bygleswurth scowled. "You should have told her sooner, Quinlan. She would have been better prepared for my true form. Now, look at her reaction. It is absolutely preposterous."

Her father grabbed her wrist. "Niamh, where are ye going?"

*"I bhfad ar shiúl!"* Far away! As far away as her feet would take her. Wrenching her arm from her father's grip, she unbuckled the seatbelt and unlocked the door. She threw the passenger side door open, stumbled out of the truck, and darted for the tall brush on the other side of the dirt road.

That *thing* hadn't just talked. She could probably deal with that, but it shifted. It didn't look like a house cat anymore. It didn't look like anything she'd ever seen before. And she'd seen some pretty interesting magical creatures in her thirteen years. Sure, most of them were shifters, but he … Bygleswurth … didn't look like any shifter she knew.

Her heart raced. Her breathing became erratic. Niamh sprinted forward. She didn't care which direction she headed, as long as it got her away from her father and that thing. Whatever it was.

"Niamh," her father called out. "Would ye stop?"

She spun around on the ball of her foot. "Ye want me to stop? He was talkin'! And changin'! And you want me to stop? Are you planning to explain what is goin' on? Because I'm losing me damn mind."

"Watch your mouth, young lady."

Her father had a lot of nerve. Sure, her parents prohibited cussing in their house. Not that it prevented her older brother from using those kinds of words every now and again. And she didn't care much about which words she used, as long as she got some answers. "I can't believe you're giving out about my language when ye haven't explained anything to me. Either give me something since you seem to know exactly what's happenin', or I'm goin' to keep walkin'."

Bygleswurth wandered up, huffing and puffing. Between heavy breaths, he muttered, "Just … tell … her."

Her father brushed a hand across his short, red hair and propped both of his hands on his hips above the sword he had strapped to his side. "This isn't how I meant to tell you, but I s'pose I don't have a choice. Niamh, you're the Guardhian to the realm of *An Talamh Beo*."

She was a what for the what? What was her father talking about? Realm? They lived in Kinvara, County Clare, Ireland. And it was on planet Earth. Her nose crinkled, and she narrowed her eyes at him. "I don't understand. What does that even mean? An' what does it have to do with 'em?"

"Please, do not point. It is quite boorish," Bygleswurth declared.

"There are nine realms. As a Guardhian for *An Talamh Beo*, you're responsible for the safety of its inhabitants. As for what all of this had to do with Bygleswurth, he is your catalync. One is given to each guardhian to serve as a guide."

Okay. That was a lot to swallow. She protected creatures in a realm that they would access from the caves. And the thing ... catalync ... that had looked like an ordinary cat fifteen minutes ago was supposed to help her with all of this. Niamh laced her fingers together behind her head and glanced between her father and the creature sitting a few feet away. She had so many questions. How was she going to protect these creatures? Where were these other realms? Was she the only Guardhian? What exactly was Bygleswurth supposed to guide her through? Why could she see and understand him now when she couldn't earlier?

"I know this is a lot to take in, but I promise I will explain it all as we head onto the entrance."

Dropping her hands to her sides, Niamh sighed. "I just don't understand why ye didn't tell me any of this sooner, Daidí."

"I thought I had more time before your powers awakened."

"Powers?"

That answered one of her questions. Definitely put a couple of things into perspective. Like maybe why she saw the red light from that man last night. Or why the black shadow around her father had returned. Or why she saw Bygleswurth differently.

"Yes. You know how I cast spells with the right words? Your powers are like that except they come from within ye."

"Is that why I see 'em?" She gestured to the catalync this time instead of pointing. No need to be rude a second time around, though it amused her how easily she could get under his skin.

"Yes, it is why you see my true form. Your first power is sight, which gives you the ability to see the world as it is, as well as auras of those around you." Bygleswurth snorted.

Niamh opened her mouth and snapped it shut. She could stand there asking questions all day, but it would only delay the inevitable. Despite the sudden change in her comprehension of how the world functioned, her father brought her out here for a reason.

It was time she abided by his original intentions. "All right. I don't enjoy having all these questions still, but you can explain on the way. Lead on."

"Are ye sure?" her father asked.

"I am."

Obviously, this wasn't a conversation they could have in a matter of minutes. And if this trek was anything like she expected, there would be plenty of time for answers.

"Good, then let's get on."

"I do not suppose you might carry me?" Bygleswurth questioned. "This is an awfully long hike and I do not believe I will make it. Also, I would get my paws dirty."

Niamh cocked an eyebrow. He was joking, right? How would she carry him with that spiked tail of his?

"Lord, I hope all catalyncs aren't like you." Her father smirked.

"Well, of course they are. Not a single one of us would abide by dirt in any manner—sweat or otherwise."

Shaking her head, she strode forward. "The exercise would do ye wonders. Ye are a lil' fat."

"I do say! Did you just call me fat? You insolent child. I am far from fat. I am merely big-boned."

"Ha! If you're big-boned, then I'm a trekasha." Her father chuckled.

"What is a trekasha?" she asked. If he was going to use these words, he really had to explain them first.

"Tree spirit, though when called upon, the trees will physically move."

"Are we finally taking a breather?" Bygleswurth panted heavily.

Niamh rolled her eyes. They had hiked for about an hour and a half or so. They had ambled through the caves for around thirty minutes. She suspected they had to be close to the entrance for the realm, given how the air had cooled down so dramatically in the last few minutes. That didn't include the water she'd noticed along the walls. Despite all that, her catalync had been hoofing it and sweating his furry, little blue-gray arse off.

"Ye could have very well lost five whole pounds, an' it took all that walking just to do it."

"Come on, we don't have much further to go." Her father readjusted the belt around his waist and waved them forward.

"Must we continue on?" Bygleswurth whined and leaned against the wet limestone, then scrunched his nose and shook out his paw.

"You're completely useless." Niamh crossed her arms and stared at her catalync. She had two choices. One, leave him there; he would catch up with them eventually. Two, pick his sarcastic behind up and carry him the rest of the way. Neither was a great option. As much as he deserved to be stuck there, she refused to leave him behind. Scrunching her nose, she picked up her catalync and hefted him up on her shoulder. "Ye just be careful with that tail."

"I shall keep it tucked away."

Sure, he would. She stood still while Bygleswurth arranged and re-arranged himself a second time. After a moment, he finally settled his bulk and carefully laid his tail across her opposite shoulder atop the short-sleeved t-shirt she had on. "Are ye done?"

"Yes. Shall we carry on?"

She groaned and ambled forward again, being careful of every step she took. One wrong move would send both her and Bygleswurth flying and falling on one of his spikes wasn't high on her priority list. They angled from his tail like wheat kernels, but unlike the grass, she bet they hurt.

"So Daidí, what were you saying about the first Guardhian?"

"The first Guardhian, the line ye get your powers from, was the child of the goddess Di'Lacia."

"How is that even possible? I thought she was a member of Tuatha-de-Danann." She had heard the story several times as a child. At least with the family of gods. They were excellent with magic, and one by one, claimed various parts of Ireland.

"She was. When she came to Ireland, they gave her *An Talamh Beo* as a gift. She intended to make it a realm all others would envy. Then she fell in love with the god Feid'Helm. He convinced her together they could make the land a thing of beauty and for some time they did."

"That sounds more like a love story than one of tragedy."

If something bad hadn't happened or an evil hadn't come lurking, there wouldn't have been a need for a Guardhian. Even she could attest to that. It was the way of the world and how every story always went.

"You're quite right. Another god, Ci'Haran, which translates to 'the dark one,' showed up. He had always loved Di'Lacia and was quite upset she turned him away. Determined to prove 'imself to 'er, he began callin' creatures to *An Talamh Beo*. That caused harm to the land, so he tried transforming the ones already there, which only made things worse."

Her eyes widened. There explained the need for an entity to protect all the work the goddess and god had done to the realm. Everything they'd given to make it spectacular and jealousy ruined it. "Is that why they created the Guardhians, then?"

"Must you continue to interrupt him? Your father is attempting to teach you about your legacy." Bygleswurth's whiskers twitched.

Niamh opened her mouth and snapped it shut. Ahead, she could see the most luscious field of green and brown and gold and blue. The trees were so tall they had no end. She might as well have been on top of a mountain because the air was so pure. The sun shined so brightly it was like bathing in the light for the first time.

There were bright and colorful birds, or so they appeared, soaring through the air. She even spotted a few white outlines of spirits dancing amongst the trees. The closer she got, the more she heard what sounded like crashing waves. Even the temperature cooled down, but nothing extreme. It was almost perfect.

Lifting the catalync from her shoulder, Niamh set him on the ground and approached what she presumed was the entrance to the realm. The moment she stepped through; a calm washed over her. Her entire body relaxed, from the top of her red hair all the way to the tip of her toes. It was the strangest and most liberating sensation.

She felt like ... she was home.

# CHAPTER THREE

Nessan lifted his nose to the air and sniffed. He'd shifted
to his bear form as it heightened his senses. After what he saw in
that prison, he needed to find the cause, and fast. It had taken a
few minutes of prodding, but Fionn had finally told him what
he needed to know.

The shapeshifter had babbled something about dark figures
with no faces when questioned upon his return to the pack
house. Within a matter of minutes, the male's words changed to
an unrecognizable language. All of that occurred an hour before
he'd arrived for his meeting with Fionn. The shifter's condition
had worsened to the point of imprisonment by the time he'd
gotten there. As if that wasn't bad enough, he watched the guy
deteriorate further. So much that he started throwing himself
against the prison walls. Medical staff had rushed in and sedated
the shifter before he caused more harm.

There he stood, attempting to catch a whiff of the shifter's
scent. It would give him a direction to go. The Barna Woods
was rather vast. Although there were other places that were
larger, he didn't want to be spotted in this part of the country.
Bears weren't commonly found out here. As he trekked forward, something stagnant wafted through the air. He wrinkled
his nose.

Good Di'Lacia that was something awful. That yoke was
completely manky, and he hadn't even approached it yet. He'd
smelled nothing like it. There wasn't a bog or anything here
that would cause a stench like this. Maybe it was whatever had
harmed the shapeshifters Fionn had sent. Or the thing several
humans had spotted.

Against his better judgment, Nessan followed the foul smell. Nothing covered it, not even the wildflowers he noticed along the way. The closer he got to the source, the stronger it got. Spotting the origin of the stench, he stopped. Twenty yards ahead, a body laid against a tall tree. Its mouth hung open at a strange angle. It looked like something out of a horror movie. Was it human? Or was it the missing shapeshifter?

One way to find out.

Nessan trudged closer until he got within a few feet of the body. Not that he'd needed to get this close to confirm its species. It was the other shifter. What the feck caused this? His fur stiffened. What he'd smelled was right on top of him. He wasn't alone.

Growling, Nessan spun and swiped at the black shadow behind him. Holy shit. The descriptions of what the humans and that shifter had seen were accurate. This *thing* had no face. It had black pits for eyes, no nose, no corporeal body. While he wasn't positive, he was fairly certain he knew what it was, not that he knew how it got here.

Shadows only appeared one way. But that wasn't even remotely possible. So, this couldn't be a shadow.

Lunging forward, he swiped his claws at it again. The creature screeched. Out of his periphery, he caught sight of another shadow approaching his position. How many of these things were there? Feck. He couldn't defeat one, let alone two. He only had one way of escape.

Nessan inhaled a deep breath and let out a loud growl. The surrounding wind pulsated, throwing the unsightly black monsters into nearby trees. It wouldn't take them long to charge him. He took advantage of the moment presented and ran. His speed in this form was much faster than his human form. He just had to close to the parking lot, then he could shift back to his human form and leave the woods.

It wasn't much of a plan, but it was all he had. At least for now. Once he confirmed his suspicion, then he'd figure the rest out.

Because only a guardhian could defeat shadows.

"How much farther is it?" Bygleswurth whimpered.

"Would ye quit complaining? It's gettin' annoyin'." Niamh quickened her pace. She had intentionally slowed down so he could keep up, but she couldn't bear any more of his complaints. First, he grumbled it was unbearably hot, and then he moaned how this was the longest hike of his life. Not to mention the number of times he asked for someone to carry him. If he continued on this exhaustive rant, she was going to shave him and figure out her powers on her own.

Her father gripped her shoulder and smiled. "This shouldn't amuse me, but it's nice to have someone else dealin' with his nonsense."

"Don't tell me he's always like this."

She'd leave him here if that was the case. Maybe that was what her catalync needed. A few nights in the forest where he had to hunt for his own food and stay warm. Niamh trekked up a hill and giggled at the thought. If she did that, she'd have to stay and watch.

"Actually, he's spent most of 'is time pushing me to tell you about your heritage."

At least somebody had been. According to her father, her mother didn't know all the details. Her brother knew nothing, but her cousin and aunt, well, they knew everything. Kind of helped that her cousin had the same heritage. Like her brother, Nessan was a shapeshifter. Like her, he belonged to the same legacy. The only difference was their link to *An Talamh Beo*. While she was the Guardhian, her cousin was the prohtector. He handled her safety.

It didn't make any sense until she understood that what she experienced now was only the beginning of her powers. The rest would develop. How long would it all take? That all depended on her, which was why she focused on as much as she could on the spiritual essence she saw around her, especially her father. Something was off with him, but she couldn't say what. Theoretically, the more she studied and learned, the quicker her powers would come. Then, whatever darkness surrounded her father, she could defeat it.

Or so she hoped.

Niamh stopped and glanced over her shoulder. As much as she imagined leaving Bygleswurth there overnight, she wouldn't actually leave him behind. "How far behind do ye think he is?"

Quinlan sighed. "I'm sure not far."

"Do ye think we should go back?"

"That depends. Are ye going to be upset with me—"

Near to where they stood, there was a loud snarl, followed by a hiss. Her father grabbed the hilt of the sword at his side and yanked it free of its scabbard. "Niamh, I need ye to run."

She shrunk back and her eyes enlarged. "But—"

"Ye run as fast as ye can go." He pointed in the direction they traveled.

With a quick nod, Niamh ran away from him. Her father took off in the opposite direction, toward the sound. She lingered for a moment until he disappeared from her sight and then darted forward. Not that she had any idea where to go. Or if there was any place to go. She didn't know the forest.

Glancing over her shoulder, she slowed her steps. All she could see was one tall tree after another. The crunch of a twig behind her sent her running. Her gaze flitted from one flickering shadow on the ground to the next. A branch scraped her skin as she ran, but she didn't care. She couldn't stop. Something chased her. She could hear their feet pounding against the ground.

Niamh peered back and ran into something hard. She stumbled backward a few steps and lifted her gaze up at the creature. Frozen in place, she trembled. With wide eyes, she gawked at the ugliest creature she'd ever seen. It stood almost seven-feet tall. What she presumed was hair hung from its head like muddy moss. It had large teeth and long claws. Dark hair covers its putrid green skin.

*Run,* she thought.

She had to run. Why wasn't she running? Why wouldn't her feet move? Sweat dripped down her back. The hair on the nape of her neck rose. No matter how hard she tried, she couldn't get her body with the program.

The thing lurched at her.

Niamh screamed.

It picked her up off the ground and tossed her over its leathery shoulder.

"Daidí!"

Where was it taking her? Why had it grabbed her? She had to do something. The synapses in her brain finally got on board with this whole escape plan. Niamh wiggled, and the creature tightened its hold on her waist. Balling up her fists, she pounded on its back and squirmed. She had to fight to get free. It gripped harder.

Her lungs burned at the restriction. Her breath came out in shallow, rapid puffs. If she continued writhing, it was only going to get more difficult to breathe. It might even kill her, though it was probably going to do that, anyway. Niamh swallowed.

She refused to die like this.

She had to fight.

She had to fight!

She had to—

Niamh felt a jolt between her and the monster.

The creature lost its grasp and dropped her. She landed on the ground on her butt. She scrambled to her feet to run when something whizzed through the air and collided with the creature's throat.

It weaved, fell forward, and hit the terrain with a loud thud.

Her heart hammered in her chest. Panting heavily, Niamh swiveled her head around. Where had the arrow come from? Did it come from behind her? In front? She couldn't tell. Someone had killed it, but who? Her father?

It couldn't have been him. He hadn't brought along a bow and arrow, only a sword. At least now she understood why. Whoever it was, they'd probably saved her life. The monster was dead now. Tears welled up in the corners of her eyes. She buried her face in her hands to collect herself. Man, she didn't want to go through that again.

A bright white light converged on where she sat.

Lifting her gaze, Niamh shielded her eyes from the light, only for it to disappear. A female replaced it.

Of sorts.

It looked like a woman but had long, white wings. Its hair was the bronze color of bark, which hung down to the middle of its back. Its eyes were as bright as emeralds. It had porcelain-toned skin and tiny ears. It stood in a white dress that flowed like the ocean.

Niamh hadn't seen anything like it before, not even in her books. What was it? Whatever it was ... it gave her a sense of peace. As if everything in her world would be all right.

"Good afternoon, Niamh. I am Grianne." She smiled and held out her hand.

She knew her name. How did she know her name? Niamh blinked and noticed the bow in the hand not being offered. Well, whatever type of creature she was, she had saved her life. That was something. Hesitantly, she placed her hand in the creature's. It was so soft. Like rose petals.

Grianne pulled Niamh to her feet. "You should be more careful when you trek through the realm. I am not ready to lose another Guardhian."

Lose another one? How was that even possible? Her father said Guardhians were born every hundred years during the re-birthing cycle. If this ... creature had been around for the last one, she had to be at least a hundred years old.

Niamh blinked. "What are you?"

"I see you are still learning things. I am a Solfhionn." Grianne strode in the direction Niamh had originally come from.

"What does that mean?"

"I believe it roughly translates to white phoenix. I would suggest speaking with your father to confirm. Has he taught you nothing of the creatures inhabiting this realm?"

"I haven't learned much of anything. Except for the history." She scanned the expanse of the forest for her father and Bygleswurth. She didn't think she had run too far. But that didn't include the distance the monster covered with her on its shoulder. They could be miles back for all she knew.

Her father came barreling through the trees. He scooped her up in his arms and spun her around. "Oh, thank Di'Lacia, you're alive."

"Yes, Daidí. I'm fine, but that does hurt."

Her side and upper abdomen were sore where the monster had squeezed. A bruise was better than dead. One would heal, the other wouldn't.

"I'm sorry." He set her down and placed a chaste kiss on her forehead. "I'm just glad you're okay."

"Quinlan ... have ... you..." Bygleswurth tried to get out between heavy breaths as he shuffled in from behind a tree.

"I see you have brought your pet along," Grianne commented.

Niamh stifled a giggle. She shouldn't laugh, but that was funny. Hmm, would things change now that she saw his true form? Or would he still expect to be pampered as he had been for the last seven years?

Catching his breath, Bygleswurth snorted. "I am not her pet. You know how much I despise that term."

"We can easily settle this. Do you sleep in her domain? Does she feed you? Take care of you? Attend to your every need?" Grianne tucked her bow beneath a wing.

"Of course; however, it was only so I could maintain the pretense of a domesticated animal." Bygleswurth flicked the hook of his tail in the air and held his head high, which caused his white chin to stick out.

Her father frowned. "Enough, Grianne. Stop teasin' 'im. There isn't time for your bickerin'. We need to get movin'."

"How many more were there?" Grianne asked.

"Three. I killed one and called the trekasha to help with the other two. And before ye ask, yes, I thanked 'em." Her father returned his sword to the scabbard at his side and gestured for them to move forward.

So many words flying around between the three of them. She hated being out of the loop. All of them understood one another and somehow, they expected her to walk on as if nothing had happened. Some monster tried to kidnap and kill her, and if she heard her father correctly, there had been something else out there.

Niamh crossed her arms. Was she supposed to fight all of this on her own? "I'm not moving until you explain a few things to me."

"There could be more coming. Let's talk about this when we get to the cabin." Her father requested.

"This can't wait. Ye push it off and push it off. You spent most of our hike here telling me 'bout the history instead of the creatures. Information I could really use." She couldn't explain what caused that monster to drop her. It was like an electrical shock that passed between them. At least that's what it felt like to her. But short of getting off its shoulder, she had no other plan. She didn't know how to kill it or even if she could. The latter was obviously a moot point now, since the arrow proved it could die. But what if the arrow had never come?

Her father propped one hand on his hip and rubbed his brow.

Uncrossing her arms, Niamh stared at the arm in front of his face. Brown and red caked his forearm. "Is that blood?"

He eyed his arm. "Ah shit, I forgot all about it."

"You forgot? How do ye forget you got hurt?"

The sight of the dried blood didn't make her queasy, but it bothered her it had gone unchecked. Yes, the realm felt like home, but it didn't mean there were healing properties in the ground.

"We can get his wound cleaned and dressed at the cabin. It is still some ways off. I shall keep a watch from overhead, while you three continue on foot," Grianne said.

It was a good plan. With one flaw. Her gaze shifted to Bygleswurth. She didn't even waste time asking. She picked him up and hefted him onto her shoulder. "Make yourself comfortable."

"I am ever so grateful," the catalync responded.

"Pet," Grianne muttered, spread her white wings wide and flew into the sky above them.

The cabin was built above ground and into the trees here. It rested on enormous trunks that had to have been carefully carved as the edges fit quite snug. It must've taken some time to build the cabin to such perfect proportions. No way had it naturally formed that way, unless the trees had grown around it, which at least part of them had with the way they formed a barrier over the roof.

Niamh cocked an eyebrow and studied the outside of the building for a moment longer. Something to ask her father about, after he'd been bandaged up.

"Will you let me down now, please?" Bygleswurth asked.

"Huh?" Niamh glanced over her shoulder. She'd completely forgotten he was even up there. It had been a couple of miles since he'd made his presence known. She crouched down, pulled her ponytail to the side and angled her back so he could jump off himself. Much easier than hefting his fat behind off.

Bygleswurth hopped down and trotted after her father and Grianne into the cabin.

No need to follow behind them. She was perfectly safe, although she couldn't fully explain why ... unless...

Niamh looked from the cabin to the tree-line behind them. To the naked eye, it appeared to be nothing more than an abundance of trees. But when she inspected it closer, she could see white shimmering through the trees and around the clearing.

It was protected.

No wonder she felt so safe from harm. Sighing with relief, she headed into the cabin and stopped in the doorway. Her skin tingled. Several colors filled the room from a muddy pink to an orange yellow to a pale yellow. What in the world had she stepped into?

"Niamh?" her father called out.

As soon as one color faded, another replaced it. It was as if someone had come into the cabin and thrown a can of mixed paint everywhere. It covered the whole place from top to bottom in a multitude of colors. She couldn't decipher one from the next. How was she supposed to interpret them all?

"Niamh. Take a deep breath."

She could barely hear him. His voice was so muffled. It sounded like when he would call out her name while she was under the water. Her eyes widened. Had she fallen into one of the waterfalls they'd hiked around? Maybe they hadn't made it to the cabin. Her pulse raced. Maybe she'd ... she was so light-headed.

*Holy shit, this is too much,* she thought.

Niamh weaved on her feet and fell to the floor as darkness claimed her.

Quinlan surged to his feet and kneeled beside his daughter. Leaning in close, he held a hand above her nostrils and then laid his first two fingers against the side of her neck. He sighed. "She just fainted."

"You should have warned her of the cabin's magic," Bygleswurth said.

"Were you not the last one with her?" Grianne asked.

Now he remembered why he hadn't been in a hurry to educate his daughter. It wasn't the main reason, but it was one of many. He scooped her up into his arms. "I'm going to lay 'er down on the bed in the back room. You should keep her company, Bygleswurth."

"Anything to get away from this treacherous angel." He flicked his tail and stuck his nose in the air as he pranced down the hallway.

"Angels do not have pointed ears, pet!" Grianne yelled.

Holding his daughter tight in his arms, Quinlan groaned and kicked the bedroom door open. "Must ye antagonize 'er?"

"No, I suppose not, though I cannot abide by her consistently downgrading my importance, either."

He laid Niamh in the bed, brushed her crimson red hair to the side and plumped the pillows behind her head. He studied the delicate features of his daughter: the freckles sprinkled across her nose, the subtle roundness of her ears, the dimple she had in her right arm. Things that easily escaped notice, but that he certainly wanted to remember. There wasn't much time left.

Quinlan dragged a hand down his face. This was the last thing that needed to happen today. He couldn't chastise the catalync like a child, but it would feel nice if he could. And he didn't dare reveal what he suspected the next few days would entail. It would happen whether he spoke of it. Maybe there was a way around that.

"Listen to me. I need ye and Grianne to get along for Niamh's sake. She's going to need you both soon enough."

Bygleswurth bowed his head and then leaped onto the bed. "I understand. I shall rise above the occasion and do what is necessary for Niamh."

"Thank ye. And don't worry. I'll talk to 'er too." Quinlan left the bedroom and closed the door most of the way. He strolled back down the hallway and sat at the round wooden table he'd previously occupied. He presented his arm once again to Grianne, who returned to cleaning the gash in his forearm. It needed to be stitched up. The grullac had gotten him good. Damn near hit the bone.

"Do you not intend to tell her?"

Grianne was one of the few that knew the truth. Not that he ever believed she'd throw it in his face. Or expect him to tell his daughter. *That* would never happen. And she had promised to keep it a secret as well. "It wouldn't do any good, an' ye know that."

"You do not know that is true. The future is only set if our actions remain unchanged."

"She just got 'er sight. If I told 'er the truth, then all I'd do is get 'er killed. She's my daughter. I couldn't stand to see that happen." It was his job as her parent to protect her, and he'd do anything in his power to keep her safe. Even if that meant risking his own life.

"I think she has gained more power than any Guardhian in the past five-hundred-years. Quinlan, she has already called an electrowave, though she may not have realized it."

He blinked. Impossible. No Guardhian got their powers that fast. There hadn't been one in history that he was aware of. The only person who would know for sure was Meara. Quinlan narrowed his eyes and frowned. "Are ye sure?"

"I am quite positive. I saw it myself. It was what caused the grullac to drop her." Grianne set aside the cleaning supplies and then dug out a needle, thread, and matches. "I am going to stitch this to prevent infection."

"Go 'head."

He really wished Meara hadn't disappeared. He could use her advice right now. Every instinct in his body flared at the mere thought of telling his daughter the dark truth. The fact remained, even if she had provoked further power, she likely wouldn't be able to do it again. That wouldn't just endanger her life, it would endanger others. No. This was one secret he was better off keeping.

Quinlan flinched as the needle pierced his skin. It had been quite some time since he had been this injured. Maybe he wouldn't survive the next one, but that was his burden to bear. "I can't tell 'er. Just remember, you promised not to say anything either."

Grianne lifted her eyes to his. "What if she is your salvation?"

"That's a chance I'll have to take." He would not risk her life to save his own. And that was the end.

# CHAPTER FOUR

Nessan opened the door to the cabin and shut it as he peered into the living room and kitchen. He folded his arms across his chest and narrowed his gaze at Quinlan. "We need to talk. Now." He'd spent the last couple of hours verifying his suspicions. Then gone on a search for Quinlan. The male hadn't been at home or the pub, which left him with one conclusion.

Niamh had finally gotten her powers.

All of which led him to the cabin. Though it irritated the feck out of him to go through all this trouble. His cousin had to make things difficult.

"It's not a grand time."

"I don't care," Nessan replied. "This is too important to shuck off." A decision had to be made and quickly regarding the shadows. Not that he expected Niamh would have the power yet to defeat the creatures. It could be weeks before that happened. Her sight would help her see them, but it wouldn't do a damn thing to aid in her fighting them.

"What the feck could be so important that it cannot wait?"

He uttered one word that would catch his cousin's attention. "Soul-snatcher." The male's gaze jerked toward him.

"Outside," Quinlan said as he stood.

Fine by him. He didn't give a shit where they talked as long as they spoke. Nessan opened the door, let Quinlan walk out first, and followed him.

"What makes ye think there's a soul-snatcher out there?" Quinlan asked.

"A shapeshifter death by a shadow. Another soon to follow if the problem isn't handled. We need to get Niamh trained an' quickly so we can deal with it." None of his research had given him an alternative. The shadows were the first sign of a developing soul-snatcher, which was also how they identified the soul-snatcher. And stopped it from gaining power.

"That's impossible. A soul-snatcher hasn't existed in hundreds of years. And no one has reported any human deaths."

"I saw 'em with my own two eyes, Quinlan. There may not be any deaths yet, but that doesn't mean we aren't on the verge of them. Niamh—"

"Has just gained her sight. She passed out from the overload of the cabin's magick. I refuse to subject 'er to the unnecessary. I don't care if ye saw 'em or not. This is my daughter, and I'll protect her in every way I can."

Nessan barely contained a growl. His cousin had unnecessarily cut him off. As much as it shouldn't piss him off, his cousin had already irritated him at having to run all over to find the male. "Niamh has a duty to protect the realm and Ireland. The sooner ye accept the inevitable, the better it will be."

"I am aware of her duty. I don't need ye to explain it to me."

"Then ye need to act like it. Train 'er. Without Meara here, that is your duty." Not that he understood why Meara hadn't started training Niamh prior to her disappearance. Unless Quinlan had objected to it. It wouldn't surprise him. His cousin had done whatever possible to keep Niamh out of a world she was born into.

"I am trainin' 'er."

"With more than just havin' 'er read books. She needs the physical skill set to go with the mental. Right now, it's what she needs more." They couldn't wait forever for Quinlan to get his head out of his arse. Too much was at stake. "Ye have twenty-four hours to start. If ye don't, I will." With that, Nessan walked off. He'd said his peace and gotten the information he required. Now, he would check in with the alpha. See where they stood with that other shapeshifter.

Niamh ran her fingers over the tome Grianne had given her before they'd left the cabin a few hours ago. She glanced at Bygleswurth curled up next to her in the front seat of her father's truck, and then to her father. Would they care if she cracked it open now? Her mind was clear.

The earlier nap had done wonders for the circuits in her brain. It was like someone had pushed an overdue reset button. She'd been able to see through the muddle of colors once she'd woken up. That allowed her to spend some time exploring the cabin. Not as much time as she would've liked, though. Still, she roamed and examined a lot.

She'd discovered a couple of chests in some of the other bedrooms. One contained tomes like the one in her lap, while the other had various maps and other items she'd never seen before. Her father hadn't let her dig around long enough to describe any of them.

Instead, he offered some creature-education. Better than nothing in her book. Turned out the monster that tried to kidnap her was called a grullac, a desolate warrior in the war for the realm; one of the dark creatures created by the god, Ci'Haran. They weren't very smart, but large and aggressive. And there were only two ways to kill them: cut off their head, which sounded like a horrible Queen of Hearts reference, or sever their cervical spine, like Grianne had done with the arrow.

She should learn how to do that. Well, shooting an arrow would be grand, but fighting period would be best. Mastering her magick as it developed wouldn't be enough. She had to defend herself. No way would her father protest against it now. Not with what happened. Though the tome was her only homework for the time being, but she could add this to the list. Right?

He'd understand.

"While we're at the pub, a friend of mine will come by for a bit. He wants to meet you, so I need you to be on your best behavior."

Cocking her head, Niamh raised an eyebrow. Had her father forgotten which child he was speaking to? She was almost always on her best behavior. Her brother was the one that caused trouble. He could find more ways to rebel than an activist.

"I'm always good."

"I need ye to be ladylike, quiet, and demur."

"Do I have to put on a dress, too?" She smirked. Ladylike and best behavior were two different things. Her mother raised her to be independent and strong, not how to keep her trap shut and bow to the desires of a man. She would never be the latter, though she could probably pretend if her father insisted on it.

"We don't have time for that. What ye have on will do."

"I was joking." Had that cut on his arm become infected or something? Maybe he'd had some juice while she slept. Or he could've snuck in a shot while she explored the cabin. Either way, he had to be out of his mind. She'd die before she ever got caught in a dress.

Her father pinched the bridge of his nose. "Sorry. I don't know what I'm saying. I'm just a wee bit nervous over the two of you meeting."

Nervous? What would he have to be worried about? This friend wouldn't cause them any harm, right? Friends were typically people you got along with; people who kept you safe and helped you figure things out. Why did she get the feeling this so-called friend was anything but a genuine friend?

Niamh played with the ends of her ponytail. "Then why do we have to meet at all?"

"Because I promised 'im he could meet ye tonight."

She opened her mouth and snapped it shut. Why bother trying to change his mind? His word was his bond. How many times had he told her that without a person's word, they had nothing? Too many to count. He'd ingrained it in her since she was wee.

Reaching across the sleeping catalync, Niamh grasped her father's arm and squeezed. "Don't worry, Daidí. I'll be polite to your *friend* and I won't speak unless I'm spoken to."

"That's my girl." Her father smiled.

Niamh closed her eyes, inhaled and exhaled a deep breath. Who knew there was so much information to learn about reading auras? There couldn't seriously be that many colors in a wheelhouse. It wasn't as simple as red meant anger or passion; she actually had to learn the difference in the shades and whether the color appeared muddy to decipher it all. And that didn't even include her magick.

Wrapping her hands around her glass, she sipped at the Club Rock Shandy she had gotten. *Ahh, a great way to wake up the brain,* she thought. It had been a long day, and she was feeling it. Part of her hoped this friend of her father's arrived soon.

She focused back on the pages of the tome. If the aura contained a dark muddy pink color, they would view the person as dishonest or immature. Her brother probably had a lot of that. He may have been a few years older than her, but he was definitely less mature. Another color of concern was a dark shade of gray. This likely meant a person—

*Ding!*

"My goodness, is that him?" Bygleswurth popped his head up from the seat next to her.

"Would you sit back down?" Niamh turned toward the front door of the pub as it swung shut.

A rather large man with rusty-colored hair and rusty-brown eyes stood in the doorway. He was chubby—all over. Sweat beaded on his forehead. His rosy cheeks were swollen and his belly was extremely round. He looked like he had a boulder under the dark gray suit he wore. His lips pressed into a thin line.

It wasn't his physical appearance that bothered her. It was the colors in his aura.

A clear red line intertwined with a muddy red ran throughout his entire aura. Not only was he a liar, he was angry, too. Then there was the thick brown running beside it. Greed wasn't an outstanding trait for a person. What concerned her most was the number of dark gray orbs scattered in his aura.

This man, whoever he was, had killed before.

Bygleswurth harrumphed, crossed his paws one over the other and lay down out of sight.

Coming from the back, her father stepped through a set of swinging doors. "Séamus. It's good to see ye."

Yeah, she was pretty sure that was a bald-faced lie. Niamh shifted her gaze back to the book in front of her. She had a lot to read and if this was the *friend* her father wanted her to meet, she honestly hoped her presence would go unnoticed.

"I know that's not true, but I'll overlook it." Séamus waddled around the bar, and a few of the high-top tables spread across the pub.

Her father nodded and gestured toward the back. "Shall we head into my office?"

"Soon enough. First, I'd like to meet this lil' girl of yours."

"Of course." Her father strode over to the booth she'd occupied for the last thirty minutes. "Séamus, this is my daughter, Niamh. Niamh, this is the friend I told ye about, Séamus."

So much for her plan to blend into the wall. Plastering a smile on her face, she slid out of the booth and stood. "It's a pleasure to meet ye, sir."

Séamus held out his sausage-sized hand. "Oh, the pleasure is all mine, Miss Niamh."

Swallowing the bile in the back of her throat, she reluctantly placed her tiny hand in his. His hand practically swallowed hers. She really didn't like this guy. If his aura hadn't told her he was a wicked man, then her sixth sense would have done the job. There was something seriously wrong with him.

He lifted her hand to his lips and placed a wet kiss on the back of it. "You can call me Séamus."

"As ye wish, Mr. Séamus." *Now, give me my damn hand back,* she thought. It took every ounce of will she had not to yank her hand from the hold he still had on her and run to the restroom so she could scrub the greasiness from his oily lips. But she was trying to do as her father had requested and act like the little lady her parents hadn't raised.

"Just Séamus." He smiled. Finally, letting go of her hand, he nodded at the book on the table. "What are you reading?"

She resisted the urge to wipe her hand on her denim shorts and instead laced her fingers together in front of her stomach. That was a ladylike move, right? And he had asked her a question, which meant she had to answer. But she couldn't tell him the truth. Or could she?

Niamh grinned. "I'm studying how to mix drinks. My father promised to let me work behind the bar when I turn sixteen. I know it's a few years away, but there's no reason not to be prepared."

"That's quite true. Does that mean you hope to take over the pub one day?"

"Yes ... Séamus. I do." It was so strange to call an adult by their first name. Even if she didn't like him. It would've been easier if he hated her speaking to him like a grown-up, then she would've done it to spite him.

Séamus glanced at her father. "Guess that means you'll have to make sure she's taught how to run a business, too."

"She's already been learning."

"Excellent." Séamus bowed slightly to her. "Niamh, if you'll excuse us, your father and I have some business to discuss."

"By all means." Niamh kept the smile on her face until they both walked away. Once they were out of sight, she unscrewed the fake grin she had plastered on her mug. At least that was over.

Quinlan turned around and led the way to his office. Yeah, he'd teach his daughter the business all right. Over his dead body. The only business she would ever learn was a legitimate one. If she wanted to take over the pub, he'd teach her the right way. Not that he was sure there'd be time for that. He'd would discreetly make a few changes to his will to ensure she received the pub. And he knew exactly how to do that.

"Your daughter is going to be beautiful when she grows up," Séamus said.

He didn't just hear that. Nope. His scumbag boss didn't just comment on his daughter's looks. Quinlan balled up his fist and stretched out his fingers. All he wanted to do was punch that pudgy arse face, but that would resolve nothing. *Do not hit him, do not hit him*, he thought to himself.

"Ye know, this has been a grand day. Truly a blessed day. First with a great business idea from your boy and then I got to meet Niamh. I see why ye dote on her so much."

His son? What could his son have come up with? And why wouldn't he have talked it over with him first? Their relationship wasn't perfect, but they worked together on a lot of things. And they always handled Séamus's business together. "What did you and Quinlan discuss?"

"Well, he had a business proposition. He believes he has a new way for me to make more money and further extend my control over the neighboring counties."

His boss didn't need more of either. Séamus already controlled Kinvara, Ballinderreen, Kilcolgan, Ardrahan, and Oranmore. Wasn't that enough? That didn't even include the port control he had recently acquired either. Even with all that, his boss hadn't mentioned what the new business entailed. Quinlan unlocked the door to his office and held it open. "What was the proposition?"

Séamus squeezed by into the office and sat at Quinlan's desk. "Your son thinks we have a shortage of sex workers in the area. An' I'm thinkin' he might be right."

There was a twinkle in his boss's pigskin-brown eyes. He knew that look and he didn't like it. It usually meant—Quinlan narrowed his eyes. *Oh, hell no.* "Forget it. My daughter is off limits."

"I would never sell 'er. She's too precious for that. No, I have other plans for 'er."

What he wouldn't give to have access to a gun right now. He'd press the muzzle between Séamus's beady little eyes and shoot. But he couldn't do that. His boss may have walked in alone, but he'd bet his pub the guy had guards standing outside.

Quinlan grabbed the bag of money and shoved it into Séamus's hands. "There are no plans. My daughter is *off limits*. Period."

"To everyone but me."

"Over my dead body."

"I can arrange that." Séamus got to his feet and strolled past Quinlan with the bag in his hands. He stopped and glanced over his shoulder. "Don't for one second think you're not expendable."

"Ye and I both know there isn't anyone who handles your money the way I do." Were there other businesses and corporations they deposited the money through to make it appear legitimate? Of course. But none of them made it happen as smoothly and as quickly as he had over the years.

"You are right. No one addresses my money the way ye do." He flashed a callous smile and left.

What did he mean by that? Quinlan frowned. Something about this whole meeting felt off. Oh, shit; everything about the meeting was wrong. From his daughter being present to the conversation afterward. He jogged through the kitchen and shoved the swinging doors open. His eyes roamed the tables and booths lined up across the floor.

Niamh sat in the same booth she'd occupied for a good hour with Bygleswurth by her side, reading the tome Grianne had given her. He waltzed over to her, extracted her from the booth, and hugged her tightly. Thank the heavens, she was still there. He placed a chaste kiss to her forehead and held her.

"Is everything okay, Daidí?"

"It's fine. I just need ye in my arms for a minute." Maybe he could protect his entire family if he moved them all to the cabin. They could hide there and give some time for this darkness to pass.

But what if it followed them?

Then what?

He hadn't thought about that before. If he took everyone there, he'd endanger all the creatures in the realm, not just his family. Okay. That wasn't his brightest idea.

There had to be something he could do. Grianne's suggestion replayed in his head. *Tell her.* That was not an option. Quinlan pulled back and caressed his daughter's soft cheek. "I need you to promise me something."

"Anything, Daidí."

"If something ever happens to me or your mum, ye run to the cabin. Ye go there and ye don't look back. Do you hear me? You don't look back." It was all he could do to keep her safe. And it hardly felt like enough.

Niamh's eyes widened and her jaw slackened. "You can't be serious?"

"Yes, I am. You promise me." It was a lot to ask of his thirteen-year-old daughter, but he'd been doing that all day. This was no different and just as important.

"Okay, Daidí. I promise."

*Nothing. There's nothing in this book.* Groaning, Niamh tossed the tome aside and flopped back on her bed. She had gone back to it after dinner. Ever since that horrible man had shown up at her father's pub, the shadow surrounding her father had returned. But the tome didn't contain a single word about what it meant.

"Please, be careful with the tome. It is an ancient text." Bygleswurth hopped up on her bed.

"Explains why it's pretty useless."

How had that book even taught Guardhians about their powers? Yeah, it had referenced a couple of things she'd be able to do within the first year of her *awakening*, and it offered a lot of detail about various auras and what the different colors meant, but it didn't have the one thing she'd been searching for.

"Perhaps if you told me what it is you were seeking, I could point you in the right direction."

She hated to admit it, but he had a point. His entire purpose was to aid her in developing her power. This was technically building her knowledge of how it all worked. Niamh sat up—

The door to the bedroom across from hers softly clicked shut.

Quietly climbing out of her bed, she tiptoed across her room and peered through the crack in her door. She hadn't closed it all the way when she'd come in earlier.

Her brother glanced toward their parent's bedroom and then crept down the staircase.

Niamh glimpsed over her shoulder at the clock on her night-stand. It was nearly one o'clock in the morning. Where was he going at this hour? She looked from the shoes by her bedroom door to Bygleswurth.

"Stay here," she whispered. She couldn't say why, but something instinctually told her to follow him. Without hesitation, she slipped her shoes on and snuck out after him.

Since he had about a sixty-second head start, she figured he had probably gone through the kitchen out the back door. It led to the barn and chicken coup on their land before opening up into woods.

Quinlan had done just that.

Using her mouth, she wet her finger and checked the direction of the wind. Her best chance of keeping out of sight was to stay downwind of him and to keep close to the barn so she could track him at a distance. Niamh ran from the barn to the windmill and hugged it closely. A large oak tree stood nearby. Once he got far enough ahead, she'd move to the tree and it would be easier to follow him unseen from there.

There was a lot of open space on their land. She and her mother hadn't gotten out to the garden yet to plant their summer vegetables.

Her brother disappeared into the woods.

She jogged over to the oak and poked her head around the wide tree. It had been on their land a long time and provided amazing cover. Niamh caught sight of her brother a good thirty feet ahead of her, but he just stood there.

What was he doing?

His body doubled over and he fell to his hands and knees. His legs shortened, then his arms shortened and his shoulders cracked. The black t-shirt and pants he wore ripped as his muscles and bones twisted and reformed. The hair on his flesh prickled out and multiplied across his entire body, forming dark red fur. His ears lengthened as the transformation from boy to wolf completed.

Good thing she hadn't moved from behind the tree. Otherwise, he would've definitely—

Sticking his nose in the air, he sniffed and peered back in her direction.

She stiffened where she stood. No way had he caught her scent. Yeah, she didn't have on any perfumes or anything, but to a shape-shifter that mattered little. She learned that a long time ago. Which was exactly why she had continued checking the direction of the wind as she made her way to the woods.

Quinlan snorted. Whatever he caught a whiff of, he must not have liked. He shook his head, pawed at his ears, and bolted deeper into the trees.

Niamh sighed. She didn't know if he'd spotted her or not. Either way, she wasn't following him now. Her powers let her see the truth about people. Yippee. Nothing in her repertoire would allow her to keep up with her brother in his wolf form.

She waited another minute to ensure he hadn't noticed her before returning home. If only Quinlan hadn't shifted. Then she would've known where he'd planned to go.

Nessan headed toward the pier. Thankfully, there weren't many harbor workers out at this time of morning. He didn't have to dart behind too many crates, so they didn't see him. The sweet smell of decay invaded his nostrils. It served as confirmation that he strolled in the right direction and gave another jolt to his senses. Slowing his pace, he ensured no one was around and disappeared down a small sidewalk. Provided he'd heard everything accurately from the alpha this morning, he should cross the body—"Holy shit," he mumbled.

Someone had sliced the male's abdomen completely open. His guts had spilled out. Blood covered the ground, pooled in a large puddle beneath the body. As if that wasn't bad enough, the eye sockets were nothing more than crispy holes. It looked like someone had taken a branding iron and burned the eyes out of the male's head. The male's mouth hung open. He'd seen nothing like this.

His ears twitched as the sound of approaching footsteps reached him. Nessan dipped to the side and pressed his back against a nearby crate.

"It's just me," Kieran whispered.

Nessan poked his head around the corner. Fionn had told him Kieran would be here. Though he expected to see him the moment he walked up. "This is bad." That didn't accurately describe the situation. He ran a hand through his hair and eyed the body. It looked like a shapeshifter had attacked the male or something similar. Not a shadow, despite the mouth. Nothing in his research referenced anything remotely similar to what he saw.

"More so than ye think." Kieran walked around, crouched down on his haunches, and gestured to the young male's mouth. "He's got no tongue."

"Shit," he muttered. "I don't even know what could've done this. It's like over one thing attacked 'im."

"Aye."

Normally, he preferred they allow the regular police to handle the situation. Under the circumstances, they needed to control the narrative. "Have ye identified the male?"

"We have not. Fionn wanted ye to see everything first before I made the call."

"Did he tell you to follow the special case protocol?" He suspected Fionn had, but he wanted to make sure. This definitely required it. Shapeshifters occupied many fields of work across the world, especially in their country.

"He did."

"Grand." Nessan eyeballed the body once more. Nothing stood out except the wounds. Whatever had done this hid it, but that didn't surprise him. He scrubbed a hand across his face. "Make the call. I'm goin' to look around the harbor."

"I will."

# CHAPTER FIVE

Niamh draped one ankle over the other and repositioned herself in the big turquoise chair in the den. She'd made herself comfortable with the tome in her lap. The double failure from the night before didn't sit well with her; she was determined to read through every line again until she discovered what the shadow meant.

Especially since she'd noticed it attached to her mother, too.

She had to figure it out, and fast.

*Knock! Knock! Knock!*

Ugh. Great. Niamh shifted in the chair and set her feet on the wooden floor.

Her mother came into the den and strode straight for the front door. "Stay where ye are. I've got it."

Worked out in her favor. As much as she didn't want to leave the comfort of the oversized chair, she would've answered the door if necessary.

Her mother opened the door. On the other side stood a stout woman with strawberry red hair wringing her hands. The woman looked familiar, but there wasn't much to note in her aura except she was overly worried. Niamh couldn't immediately place her, so she studied her face a little closer. What stood out were the woman's sea-green eyes, and the freckles sprinkled across her cheeks. They matched the facial features of one of her brother's friends. She must be the friend's mother!

"Hi, Dava. I'm sorry to bother you, but I was wonderin' if you or Quinlan Junior have seen or heard from Blaine," the woman said.

"Mairéad, I'm afraid I haven't, but come on in and I'll get Quinlan Junior. I know those two are always runnin' off and doin' something." Her mother stepped away from the door and disappeared down the hall for a minute.

Niamh half dropped her gaze back to the tome in her lap. That was where her brother had gone last night. He'd probably snuck out to go meet his friend. Then again, that didn't make any sense. Their parents wouldn't have cared if he'd gone to hang out with Blaine. The only non-magical her brother hung out with was one of the few normals their parents liked.

She'd seen him around the house a few times. As far as she recalled, he was okay. He'd always been nice to her whenever he'd come by. Lifting her eyes back to the woman hovering by the door, Niamh offered a polite smile. "I'm sure my mum will be back soon."

"Of course." Mairéad returned the smile and turned to look over the pictures on the wall.

No doubt her mother had to go upstairs to fetch her brother. Over the last couple of years, he'd become more difficult and pretentious, as if they were lucky to have him in their family. It made her wonder if her father really wanted her brother to have his namesake. But that was their tradition. Just like they named her after her mother's mother, they named her brother after her father's father. Her grandfather, father, and brother all had the same name: Quinlan.

Her mother stepped into the den with her brother in tow. "My apologies, Mairéad. I had to pop into the kitchen for a moment."

Niamh cocked an eyebrow. She didn't need to see her mother's aura to tell that was a lie, but the muddy pink color stared her in the face. It was just like her mother to cover for her brother's laziness.

"I understand. Ye have to tend to your family," Blaine's mother said.

Covering her mouth with her hand, Niamh stifled a snicker. No way had anyone with ears missed the sarcasm in that response. She didn't blame the woman. She *was* there searching for her son.

"I do, but I stopped to check with my husband to see if he had seen your son about the house," her mother said.

Quietly, Niamh closed the tome. She wanted to make her presence wee and unnoticeable. Normally, she wasn't the kind to go earwigging, but she had to listen in as this travesty unfolded.

Mairéad's shoulders slumped. "I'm sorry, Dava. I'm just worried about my boy. He didn't come home from work last night and you're my last hope of findin' 'im."

"Jesus, Joseph, and Mary, why didn't ye say anything?" Her mother took Mairéad's hands in her own. "'My husband hasn't seen him and Quinlan here hasn't either."

"I thought you both went off yesterday morning," Blaine's mother said.

"That we did, Mrs. O'Brien, but that was the last time I saw 'im," her brother said.

Niamh's eyes narrowed. That wasn't true. His aura told her so. Why would her brother lie about that? She opened her mouth to call him out on the lie when she saw it.

A dark gray orb.

No. That wasn't possible.

Her brow creased. She rubbed her eyes and checked again.

The dark gray orb remained.

And a shadow appeared.

Niamh sat at the round table in the kitchen with her chin in her hands. She'd been there for a good hour. Maybe longer. She had no clue what to do about what she'd seen.

Had her brother killed someone?

If he did, was it a norm? Something that was forbidden with shapeshifters. Unless he'd been forced to defend himself. But if that were the case, would the orb still have been there? The tome offered no information about orbs. And she wasn't certain she should ask Bygleswurth about it. Yes, he was her guide, but this was her brother.

Not to mention the whole shadow she had seen in every member of her family now. All she had deciphered was that something was coming for her loved ones.

But she didn't know what.

Or when?

The door to the kitchen opened. "Niamh, what are you doing hiding in here?"

She glanced over at her father and leaned back in the chair. There was a lot she didn't know. Even if she knew what to expect, she had no way of defeating it. "I'm not hiding. I'm thinking."

Her father headed to the refrigerator. "About?"

"Fighting." Niamh crossed her arms. She could tell him everything she had thought about for the last hour, but truth be told, it came down to her ability to protect her family. It also meant she'd be able to fulfill her duty to the realm, too.

His head snapped in her direction. "What would ye be thinkin' about that for?"

"Because I need to learn to fight." Maybe she should've brought this up another way, but he had asked. All she'd done was answer.

"There's no reason for you to know any of that."

Her nose crinkled and her eyes narrowed as she stood. *No reason to learn.* With everything that had happened in the last twenty-four hours, she had every right to learn how to fight. It would complement the powers that would grow and even give her what she needed to control them. Her father had to know all of this. "Daidí, you realize me learning to fight is inevitable, right? My powers are only going to make it necessary. As well as my duties."

"Shh." He grabbed her arm and tugged her through the dining room into his office, then shut the door. "Ye can't talk about that where everyone can hear."

They were in their own home. There had been one visitor, and she had left a while ago. Who else did that leave? "Everyone who? Only mum and Quinlan are here."

"And they don't know about your powers. It needs to be kept that way."

That made absolutely no sense. Why would it be a tremendous secret? Especially from family. She could've sworn he had told her that her mother was aware of her powers, just maybe not to the full extent. Then again, she didn't know the full extent of her powers. "I thought ye said mum knew."

"I told you, she knows you're special, but nothing more."

"Well, why can't we tell 'er? I mean, she knows Quinlan is a shapeshifter. Why wouldn't we tell 'er about me?" She suspected there were rules about who could be told what. The same thing applied to shapeshifters. Obviously, most non-magical or norms weren't told about their existence, but that didn't mean they kept families or kin in the dark. Of course, there were always stories told around a bonfire.

Those didn't include the myths in their history surrounding Laignech Fáelad or Airitech, who had three daughters, all of whom transformed into wolves. The tales spun around a good bonfire were always based on the truth. She had joined a local pack occasionally and listened intently to those stories. There had to be tales like that in her own legacy.

"Because it keeps you both safe. You're the only Guardhian in this realm. Unlike your brother, if ye die, there isn't another that can take your place. You have a greater responsibility than your brother ever will. It is imperative we keep your abilities a secret. Do ye understand?"

"I do. An' given all that, don't you think it makes sense for me to learn to fight?" Niamh crossed her arms. It was like he presented her case for her and hid behind it all at the same time. If it was so important to keep her *existence* a secret, then she had to learn how to defend herself against her enemies.

"All ye need to know right now is how to use the powers you currently have."

Why? Why was he giving her such a hard time? This darkness was going to come and she wouldn't be able to do anything to stop it at the rate he was going. She had to get him to realize how that ended. "But Daidí—"

"But nothing. I have given ye my decision."

With a groan, she threw her hands up in the air, stormed out, and slammed the office door shut.

Sighing heavily, Quinlan pinched the bridge of his nose and leaned against his oak desk. If it had been up to him, he would've delayed the awakening of her powers for a little longer. But he had as much control over that as he did his daughter.

A second door slammed close. He flinched. Likely the kitchen door from the sound of it.

"You realize this is a battle you will not win," Bygleswurth said.

"Good Di'Lacia, where did ye come from?" Quinlan jerked back.

Bygleswurth canted his head and draped one paw over the other as he made himself comfortable on the couch. "Technically, the hallway, but that was perhaps ten minutes ago."

"You could warn a person."

For as fat as the catalync was, he could be stealthy when so desired. He hated how often the creature startled him. Especially since Bygleswurth looked like a cat to everyone except him for a while. He'd been honestly surprised his son hadn't been able to see the catalync's true form. Although, the more he thought about it, the less it made sense. His son was a shapeshifter or other worldly, so he should've been able to see Bygleswurth's actual form. Unless they had never crossed paths.

Quinlan frowned. It was a big house. And the catalync ... most of the time stayed out of sight. Unless he bugged him like he was now. How did he get him off the couch and out of his office?

"I could, but if you had known I was here, you may not have been so open with Niamh regarding her learning to fight."

"She has her powers—"

"Which takes time to develop. You and I both know this. As well, she will require physical prowess as her powers grow. Otherwise, she cannot control them. Is that what you want?"

He hung his head and gripped the nape of his neck. What he wanted was for his little girl to be safe from harm. Not a life fighting the darkness consistently trying to take over the realm. She was supposed to date boys he didn't like, graduate and go on to college, eventually marry a man he questioned but ultimately approved of, get her dream job and one day far in the future have children of her own. "Of course not."

"Then perhaps you should reconsider your stance."

"It's not that simple." At least in his opinion it wasn't simple, but reality disagreed with him at all points. Grianne had fought with him over his refusal to clue his daughter in on what he suspected was coming. Now this. He was getting it from all angles.

"On the contrary. You are the only one making it complicated. I understand you are seeing this as her father, but you must see this as what is best for all of us. We depend on her to protect us. If you continue the path you have taken, she will not survive the storm."

Quinlan narrowed his eyes at Bygleswurth. He knew. He had to know. There was no other reason for him to speak of a hypothetical storm if he didn't know. Damn it! "Grianne told ye, didn't she?"

"She did not give me details, but she made me aware that you had a vision. Both Grianne and I believe you received it as a warning and that we can prevent it."

"But neither of you can comprehend the expense."

He hated that Grianne had even mentioned his nightmare. The first time he had it had been so long ago, but then it reappeared in his dreams about a month before Niamh's thirteenth birthday. Now it was all he could think about.

*He stared down the unpaved road at the blaze consuming the two-story house his grandfather had built with his own two hands. There had to be something he could do to stop this. He reached toward the house. His eyes widened. His hand crumbled into thousands of dark gray grains of dust. It took over his whole body, and the wind blew him away.*

*That's when he heard the screams. They sounded so far off, but they were right beside him. Two of them. They were both in the house. Both swallowed by the same inferno. The deathbed where he stood and watched—it was his own.*

"You cannot believe you will risk her life to save yours."

The catalync really had spoken to Grianne. Quinlan frowned. She had promised to keep their conversation a secret. No one was supposed to know what he had dreamed of or what he didn't plan to do about it. It didn't matter; he had decided. He wasn't sacrificing his daughter. "I'm not discussin' this anymore with ye."

"Very well." Bygleswurth hopped down. "Though you should know, Niamh may already be aware something is coming. She has had her own vision and your aura could have betrayed your secrets."

His face scrunched up. He hadn't considered what her sight might have revealed about the nightmare he had had, or if it would've shown her anything at all. Wait, had the catalync said something about Niamh and a dream? "What are ye talkin' 'bout? What did she see?"

"You should ask her." Bygleswurth flicked his tail and strolled out of the office.

Niamh paced from one side of her aunt's living room to the other. It was a decent sized living room easily filled with one long blue couch, two oversized, rusty orange chairs, and a coffee table. Everything needed for a family gathering or, in this case, a meeting. Hell, they could consider it an intervention.

She hadn't been able to stay in her house, so after her argument with her father, she'd gone to her aunt's place. Maybe her aunt would teach her since her father refused. Or she could talk some sense into the old man. "He doesn't get it!"

Ainsley tucked one long, tan leg beneath the other and ran her fingers through her almond-colored hair. She twisted her hair and pulled it up into a messy bun. "Ye have to see it from his point of view." She held her hand up and stopped Niamh from interrupting. "He's just worried about you, but he knows what ye need. Give 'im some time. He'll come 'round."

Time? Right. Time. The one thing she wasn't sure they had. She eyed the woman she called an aunt. Ainsley was actually her second cousin, but it was easier to identify her as an aunt. Her father had shown her their family tree to link up their lineage. One of the few things he'd been willing to teach her.

Niamh smirked. History, book stuff ... it was all great, but gammy. That wasn't entirely true. It was useless. The tome she'd read had given her some information, not much of anything for how far her powers could advance, just what she could expect within the first year of their awakening. Apparently, she'd be able to do something with electricity. But she had to focus on them now. Not a year down the line.

She really wished she had found something ... anything about the shadow she kept seeing. Would've been nice if the tome had told her more about those orbs too. She still didn't know what to make of what she'd seen in her brother's aura earlier. "What if we don't have time?"

"What do you mean?"

Shifting her weight from one foot to the other, Niamh stopped pacing and wrung her hands. Should she tell her about the shadows? Or the orb? Or both? She needed to talk to someone about it. Someone who understood this world. Because she hardly knew anything. "I can't explain it, but I keep seein' a shadow around my family. My mum, dad, brother—all of 'em; it's like something is going after 'em. An' I don't know how to stop it."

"A shadow? Are ye sure?" Nessan asked.

That had been the first word she'd heard from him in about thirty minutes. He hadn't adjusted his lanky body once. He hadn't brushed his espresso brown hair out of his face. He'd been sitting quietly in that orange chair the whole time she ranted about her father and how much he didn't want her to know.

The first mention of a shadow and suddenly he was interested. She didn't like that.

Not. One. Bit.

Niamh glanced from Nessan to Ainsley, who had also perked up. This wasn't good. "I'm certain. Why?"

She watched the two of them exchange a silent look with their matching tawny-brown eyes. They had their own secret way of conversing, like she and her father shared. But she wanted in on the secret. This had to be how Bygleswurth felt being left out of the conversation. "Why does it matter?"

Ainsley stood. "I'm going to go talk to your father about this. You don't worry about fighting. We'll get ye taught."

"Wait, what? Two seconds ago, you're telling me to give 'im time, now you're going to talk to 'im? What changed? Is it the shadows I saw? What does it mean?" She was so tired of being left with more and more questions and getting no answers. Maybe it was a good thing she didn't bring up the orb.

"All I'm going to say is that shadows are a bad omen. Now, I'm going to go talk to your father." Offering no further information, Ainsley strode out the front door.

Great. It was an answer, but an incomplete one. Bad omen could mean several things. Did it mean her family was marked for death? Did it mean they were being hunted? Neither one sounded pleasant. But she could fight both. *If* she had a bit more information. If they weren't going to provide her with it, she had one other option. Niamh shifted her gaze to her cousin. "Ye can drive, right?"

"Yes. Why?"

"Because I need to go to *An Talmah Beo*. I need to see Grianne." No reason not to give him the reason. He'd end up escorting her, whether she told him. He was her prohtector.

Nessan ran a hand across the top of his untamed hair. "Fine, but you're not going dressed like that and you're not going unarmed."

She eyed the denim shorts and t-shirt that had become her staple choice of clothing every summer. Nothing she wore could be construed as offensive. It was practically the same thing she'd worn the day before. "What's wrong with what I have on?"

"It offers no protection. If ye want to go, then ye have to change." He got to his feet.

Kind of defeated the purpose of asking him to take her if she had to go back home first. Niamh groaned and dragged her hands down her face. "It'll take time for me to go home—"

"I didn't say ye had to home an' change. I just said ye had to change. We've got something for ye here. I think it's time ye wore it." He headed toward the back of the house.

It would've been nice if he'd just said that first. Niamh jumped to her feet and followed him.

Niamh gawked at the new entrance Nessan recommended they take. It had been much faster than the path she'd taken with her father. Although according to her cousin, the reason it was less traveled had been because it put them awfully close to the swamp where grullacs lived.

Joy.

At least the clothes her cousin had her put in provided some protection. She had on a pair of brown leather pants, a pair of brown lace-up boots, a green off-the-shoulder top, and a tank-style corset. The pigtails she'd worn didn't work very well, so she traded it out for a single braid. The bottoms and top fit as perfectly as the gauntlets covering her arms and the holster around her waist. She'd even been okay with the weight of the dagger.

If only she knew how to use it.

"We're about five clicks west of the cabin," Nessan said.

"Which means what?" Did he think she had a map built into her head? She didn't know how far that meant they had to go.

"Oh brother, Uncle Quinlan really has taught ye little. It means we're roughly three miles out."

That was a lot of ground for them to cover. Walking, they'd get there in an hours' time, maybe longer. If what Ainsley said about shadows was true, they needed to get to Grianne faster. Niamh bit the inside of her cheek. She could always ask Nessan. He might know. "Do ye know anything about auras?"

"Not much. My mum thought it was best I focus on my duty to you. So, she didn't teach me a lot about them. Why do ye ask?"

She didn't want to call out her brother, either for his blatant lying or the singular orb in his aura. However, she could be general in her response. "I saw orbs in a person's aura yesterday, but I couldn't find a full explanation of 'em in the tome Grianne gave me."

"Yeah, I don't know anything about orbs. Grianne is definitely the one to talk to. Being nearly five-hundred-years-old, I'm sure she'll know."

"Five hundred? She's been here almost half a millennium? How is that even possible?" Certainly explained a few things. The comment she had made about previous Guardhians since they were born about once a century. How she seemed to move without touching the ground. Or even how she knew exactly what tome was to be read first.

"The typical life span of a solfhionn is five to six hundred years. It all just depends on the realm. They are the heart of it."

Absolutely ridiculous she didn't know any of this. And it all sounded super important. She'd almost swear her father was trying to keep her—the hairs on the nape of her neck rose. Coming to a standstill, Niamh surveyed the trees surrounding them.

Nessan stopped. "What is it?"

She couldn't respond. Not until she figured out how. Something was out there, but what? She hadn't heard anything, only felt it.

Darkness was coming at them.

Two red and black auras were running in their direction, one from each side. She'd seen those same auras the day before.

Removing the dagger from the sheath at her side, she looked at her cousin. "You need to shift. Now."

"Remember, you're small. Use that to your advantage. An' stab 'em in the throat." Nessan shucked his leather jacket and tossed it over to a nearby tree. His body doubled over and he fell to his hands and knees. His calf and knee came together and lengthened, then his arms grew and his shoulders cracked. The wife-beater and leather pants he wore shredded as his muscles and bones twisted and altered. The hair on his flesh prickled out and multiplied across his entire body as every part of him increased in size. Brown fur covered him all over. His ears shortened as the transformation from boy to bear completed.

And not a second too soon.

Two grullacs advanced on them.

# CHAPTER SIX

USE HER HEIGHT TO her advantage; sure, no problem. Total crap, HUGE problem! She dodged another swipe of the grullac's claws. She hadn't been able to get in a single strike. And she didn't even know how to call on her powers or even the tree spirits her father had gotten aid from the day before.

This creature had to have a weak spot beside its neck. What was the one place her mother always told her to go for on a guy? These things were male. Or so she assumed. Yeah, it had long moss-like hair, but it only wore a leather cloth over its nether-region. That meant it had to be male.

What had her mother said? Oh! Right! *Kick 'em in their crotch.* The two and half foot height difference didn't make that probable. She had a dagger though, and the skin was more than likely to be thinner there than anywhere else.

Without giving it any further thought, Niamh ducked the arms coming at her. She lunged forward, thrust her dagger in the grullacs's pelvis and yanked the blade back out.

The grullac howled and stumbled backwards.

She heard a roar behind her. Niamh spun around and braced herself for an impact, but the noise had come from her cousin, Nessan.

In his bear form, on his hind legs, he stood taller than the grullac. It made him a formidable opponent. Nessan swiped at the—a pair of leathery arms came around her and squeezed. *Shit!* She'd been so focused on Nessan's fight; she'd forgotten all about her own. The constriction of the surrounding arms forced her to drop the dagger.

Her arms throbbed as the grullac continued to tighten its hold around her body. She tried to push back, but she wasn't physically strong enough. Niamh screamed as the burning sensation traveled from her arms to her lungs.

It was getting harder to breathe.

She couldn't die like this.

Niamh wheezed, trying to draw air into her lungs.

*No ... air...*

*I ... can't...*

*I ... can't ... die.*

*I ... won't ... die.*

*I. WON'T. DIE!*

Her eyes rolled back, and a spark ignited from somewhere within. She couldn't say how it happened, just that a white current surged over her entire body, from head to toe.

The grullac cried out and collapsed to the ground.

There wasn't a lot of time for her to react, think, or even analyze what had just occurred. Coughing, desperately trying to catch her breath, Niamh scrambled to her feet, snagged her dagger and hovered over the grullac.

Smoke emanated from its head. It smelled a bit like charred pork, which meant it stunk.

Was it dead? Had she already killed it?

The creature flinched, and without hesitation, she stabbed it directly in the throat.

Something snorted behind her.

Panting heavily, Niamh pulled the blade out, now coated in green, and hopped to her feet. She stared at the brown bear in front of her.

Green goo covered her cousin's maw, too. It could be blood. She couldn't see the grullac he'd been fighting anymore.

Nessan glanced over his shoulder at his back.

Her eyes widened and her jaw slackened. He had to be joking. That or she imagined the gesture.

Then he lay down.

Apparently, neither applied. Niamh returned the dagger to its sheath. She wasn't keen on the idea of climbing aboard his back, but it would make their trek go by a lot faster. Before she did, she had to be certain. "Are ye sure?"

His head went up and down.

Niamh mounted his back. How was she supposed to hold on? Nessan didn't give her any time to figure it out. He rose to his full height, picked up his leather jacket in his maw and galloped through the forest.

Niamh poured hot water from the kettle into her mug and added in a bag of tea to steep. She and Nessan had arrived at the cabin roughly ten minutes before. He'd gone to one bedroom to put on fresh clothes while she meandered about the kitchen.

She'd stumbled on the tea, which seemed like a good idea given what she had endured. The thought of taking any life, evil creature or not, didn't sit all that well with her. Not to mention, she hadn't quite figured out what had emanated from her body.

The front door opened. Grianne stepped through and stopped in the doorway. She canted her head at Niamh. "Are you ill?"

"Depends on your definition."

Physically, no. Her stomach had settled within a few minutes of their arrival in the clearing around the cabin. She was fairly positive that had to do with the ride there more than anything else. Spiritually, she very well could be.

"If you are not ill, then you do not wish to drink that tea." Grianne closed the door and headed into the kitchen.

Her shoulders slumped as she sat down. "I s'pose that means it'll make me sick."

"The herbs can be difficult on the stomach if there is nothing for them to address." Grianne returned to the table and held out another bag. "Here. Try this one instead. It will settle your nerves."

"Am I that easy to read?" It couldn't be that hard to tell. Her ponytail was a little off. She had wisps of red hair all over the place. Niamh pulled the hair tie from her hair and brushed her fingers through it.

Sitting down, Grianne tucked her wings around the chair and made a new mug for Niamh. "I can feel the worry on your heart. For most, my features will shift based on those feelings. I will appear to norms, I believe you call them, as what is true in their heart. Usually their true love."

"Then how do ye feel my concern? And why do I see ye in your true form?" She realized almost as soon as she'd asked her second question that she already knew the answer. It was her sight. The same reason she saw Bygleswurth's true form.

"Because your heart is drowning in it. As for my form, your power allows you to see that." Grianne nudged the fresh mug of tea toward Niamh. "Drink."

She lifted the mug to her lips and sipped the steaming tea. *Wow!* The tension in her shoulders released. Her neck muscles loosened. Slowly, the stress ebbed from her body. She savored another sip of the tea. She couldn't say for sure, but she thought she tasted a hint of chamomile and lavender, maybe a touch of honey. There was something else, but she couldn't put her finger on it.

"Better?"

"It is. What all is in this? I think I've figured most of it out, but there's one herb ... I just don't know." She suspected there was likely a bit of magic in it, too. No tea she had ever drunk before had eased her so quickly.

"Tulsi leaves. It works rather well for relieving stress. Now that you have calmed some, do you wish to tell me what has caused such a burden?"

Where did she begin? The shadows? All she knew about them was that they were a bad omen. Or the orb in her brother's aura? She hadn't discussed that with anyone. It might be the place to start. "How much do ye know about auras?"

"A fair amount. Your predecessors taught me well."

"I met a man yesterday who had dark gray orbs in his aura. From what I read in the tome you gave me; it means they've killed. Can ye get more specific on it?" No part of what she'd said was a lie. She had phrased it that way in case Grianne could sense a lie. She wasn't certain she could or couldn't. It was best she played it safe. Niamh swallowed more of the tea.

"It means that person has taken the life of a non-magical being."

Niamh lowered the mug from her lips. Her eyes widened. Oh, this wasn't good. Not good at all. Unless it only applied to a normal? "So, I should only see them in the aura of a norm?"

"No. You may see it in a non-magical or magical being." Grianne narrowed her eyes. "Niamh, have you seen an orb in the aura of a magical creature?"

Dropping her gaze to the floor, she drank from the mug and shook her head. She hoped it covered the shock that broke out across her face. Her brother. Her older brother had committed a crime forbidden to any shapeshifter. She had been to enough bonfires to know the rules.

Interact with normals, protect them.

Do not breed with them.

Do not reveal your identity to them.

Do not kill them.

This was bad. Terrible.

Niamh's head snapped up; her shoulders hunched and her jaw dropped. Oh god! What if this had something to do with the shadows? "What about shadows? Ainsley said it was a bad omen, but I got the sense it means more."

Grianne's back straightened. "You have seen shadows in auras?"

"Yes. My whole family." Maybe she should clarify it didn't include her cousins, but whatever affected her affected them. Plus, this way she might actually get the entire picture. Someone might actually tell her what was happening.

Grianne bolted from the chair and paced from the dining room to the living room, and then back again. "Everyone? Not just your father?"

"All of them. My father, mum, and my brother." Setting the mug on the table, Niamh jumped to her feet and stood in front of the solfhionn. "Grianne, why does it matter?"

"It means they have been marked for death."

Niamh gasped. Her entire body trembled from her head to her toes. That was definitely a bad omen. And one she refused to come to pass. She could prevent it. She had to believe that.

"I can't believe ye told 'er." Nessan smirked. Freshly dressed in a pair of leather pants and a new wife-beater, he stood halfway down the hallway.

"She has every right to know," Grianne said.

"Ye know Quinlan didn't want 'er to know. None of it. Not even the other things happen' around here. He wanted to protect 'er from all of it," Nessan replied.

Steadying herself, Niamh shook her head. Her father controlled what she'd been told? Why didn't that surprise her? Getting between Grianne and Nessan, Niamh narrowed her eyes. "That's total shit and ye know it! I don't need to be protected like a wee one."

"But you are wee! Don't think because you beat one grullac that you're ready to take on something this big."

Balling up her fists, Niamh glowered at her cousin. The hair on the nape of her neck stood on end. She had never been so insulted. She wasn't that short and she sure as hell wasn't spineless. Yeah, the first time she'd seen a grullac, it scared her, but those things were horrific. It still didn't stop her from trying to escape.

"I'm a Guardhian an' if that isn't enough, then I say I'm an O'Callaghan and nothin' can stop me from tryin' to save my family."

"Ye can't even protect the normal. How do ye expect to save your family? Your sight will tell ye the darkness is coming, but it won't help you stop it. Like I said, you're wee, and ye can't change that."

"I am NOT wee!" Slamming her clenched fists in the air, Niamh emphasized the last two words. White currents shot from her fists, hit Nessan in the chest and knocked him to the ground.

Quinlan opened the door to the cabin just as Nessan flew backwards and landed on his rear. He looked from his daughter to Grianne and back to his daughter. Had she really executed her first true power? Yeah, it was against her own cousin, but he swore he saw it. He glanced over his shoulder to Ainsley, who lingered behind him. "Did ye see that?"

"If you're talking 'bout the electricity your daughter just fired, then yeah. I saw it."

That was exactly what he'd referred to; good to know he hadn't imagined the whole thing. "You should go check on your son."

Grianne had placed a hand on Niamh's shoulder and tugged her off to the side. "Deep breath."

Stepping across the threshold, he walked toward Grianne and his daughter while Ainsley headed down the hall to attend Nessan. He wasn't entirely sure what they missed, but he could at least attest to one thing. His daughter's powers had developed far faster than he expected. As much as he despised that she'd taken off, maybe it had been the right call.

"Good. One more," Grianne said.

Niamh inhaled and exhaled again, as instructed. "I feel better." Her gaze shifted in his direction. "Daidí, when did you get here?"

"In enough time to see your cousin get thrown on his arse." Sighing heavily, Quinlan hugged his daughter. He was grateful she was okay. The entire way here, all he could think of had been the worst potential outcome. She'd try to get here on her own and wind up dead.

"I didn't mean to hurt 'im, but he kept callin' me wee an' I'm not wee."

He chuckled. Loosening his grip, he cupped her soft cheek and stared into those emerald green eyes of hers. Quinlan blew out a heavy breath. He hated to admit it, but Ainsley was right. They had to train Niamh. To him, she would always be wee, but that wouldn't stop her from growing or displaying courage when he lacked it.

"No, you're not. You're the bravest person I know."

Ainsley and Nessan ambled down the hallway toward them.

Quinlan grinned and shuffled Niamh so she could see her cousin's approach. "Don't worry. He's still in one piece."

His brown hair stuck out in various directions. Smoke rippled from the top of his head. Nessan held his hands up as if surrendering. "I'm sorry. You're definitely not wee."

"I'm sorry, too. I let my anger get a hold of me," Niamh said.

"Which is why we're going to train ye to get control of that." Ainsley crossed her arms.

"Really?" Niamh glanced at Quinlan.

He nodded. Despite his desire for her not to grow up, he couldn't refute the obvious. Not to mention the burn marks he had seen on the grullac he and Ainsley passed on their way to the cabin. No way to deny it now. "Yes, especially after what we just witnessed. I can't argue with what's in my face. I think if you can find the courage to put your own fears aside to protect others, I can, too."

Grianne beamed. "I told you she was special."

"That she is," Quinlan contended. Just how much? Well, they would find out soon enough.

"Can we talk for a moment?" Nessan asked, gesturing for them to step outside.

They'd disagreed briefly the day before, not that he imagined they needed to continue that conversation privately. Though his cousin probably had to update the alpha. Quinlan nodded. He flicked his gaze to the two women in the group. "Ainsley, Grianne, why don't ye take Niamh to the back an' get 'er fitted with a bow an' quiver?"

"We can do that," Ainsley responded.

He watched as the three females disappeared down the hall, and then he and Nessan stepped outside. "Tell the alpha that we've started 'er trainin'—"

"You need to push 'er," Nessan stated, blatantly cutting him off. The male's eyebrows furrowed. "Time is runnin' out, Quinlan. This is no longer just about our world."

"What are ye talkin' 'bout?" He didn't want to speed up her training too much. It could do more damage than good. A guardhian's powers came in slowly, so they were mentally prepared to handle the responsibility. While Niamh had shown great maturity, it didn't mean they could prepare her for what would come.

"We found a normal dead this mornin' by the local port. There's a lot we don't know yet, but I don't want to take any chances. Ye need to push 'er, just like I did."

Quinlan rubbed his eyes and bit back a groan. It made sense that his cousin had forced Niamh's hand on purpose. A dead human drew a lot of unwanted attention. Of course, they'd put it on his daughter to figure out what happened. Unless the shapeshifters believed the shadows had something to do with it. Except it wasn't possible for a soul-snatcher to be developing. They were the only ones who could summon shadows. Either way, it sounded like he had little choice in the matter. "Fine, but on one condition. Ye don't mention anything to Niamh about a soul-snatcher." It would be years before she'd be ready for something so dangerous.

"I can do that," Nessan agreed.

"Good." At least that was one less thing he had to worry about. Not that it would last.

"You're releasing too soon," her father said.

"How can you even tell?" Niamh scowled and wiped the sweat from her brow. The target resembled a sieve. They had been at this for hours, with her shooting arrow after arrow at the same target.

"Because I'm watching your hold and I keep seeing the same shift."

"I can't do this anymore with you." Hanging the bow on her back, Niamh headed toward the front door of the cabin. All she felt was the wet corset against her skin. Sweat completely soaked it.

"Where are ye goin'?"

"To take a break," she half-tossed over her shoulder. Though she wouldn't mind a steaming hot shower and a fresh change of clothes, she'd accept a few minutes of rest.

She didn't expect training would be this grueling. Her shoulder burned, her biceps ached, and her fingers were numb. How did her cousin survive going through all of this? Oh yeah, he was a shape-shifter. No. That couldn't be it. He hadn't gone through his first change until he was ten-years-old. It had been the same with her brother.

So, how had her cousin gotten through the training? Unless it had been different for him. Maybe they geared it for his role. Niamh climbed the staircase and opened the front door. Her sweat had even saturated the back of her pants.

"Ye looked good out there, but Quinlan's right. Ye keep dropping your shoulder." Nessan brushed some of his hair from his face.

"Don't listen to either of 'em. You're doing good for your first time. Here; have a seat an' relax for a moment." Ainsley pulled out a chair.

At least one person was on her side. Surely, in time, they had all dragged themselves up those stairs the same way she had. Training couldn't be this hard for just her alone. Right? Or was she truly weak? Niamh laid her forehead against the round wooden table and groaned.

"Ye get five minutes an' then we need to get back out there," her father said.

Had he lost his mind? A five-minute break for hours' worth of work? That was unacceptable. She bolted upright. "Five minutes! I need thirty. You have worked me to the bone already. I need ye to give ma head pace."

"Give her some time to rest. You can't expect full of the blade her first time out," Ainsley said.

"This isn't any different from what we went through with Meara. She didn't take ages to teach us what we needed to know. My daughter should learn the same way." With a heavy sigh, her father rubbed his eyes and propped up against the wall near the table. He wiped his hands down the front of his jeans.

"Yeah, we did, but Meara isn't the one teaching Niamh. We are." Ainsley leaned back in her chair and crossed one leg over the other.

Was she supposed to know the person they were talking about? Niamh regarded Nessan. He sat there with his arms crossed and his eyes closed. Was he asleep? She doubted that. He was probably bored, which meant he knew exactly who they'd mentioned. Per usual, she was the last to know. "Who's Meara?"

"Technically, she's your trainhor. She's the one who should teach ye all about our lineage, history, fighting techniques, and your magick," her father said.

"I thought Bgyleswurth was s'posed to teach me about my powers." Niamh raised an eyebrow. That's what they had told her, right? Or had they used another term? She replayed the conversations they'd had in the last twenty-four hours.

"Well, no. He's your guide. It's his job to help direct you and point ye in the right direction. Meara should teach you the rest, but she kind of ..." Ainsley paused, "... disappeared."

"Disappeared? How?" That seemed like something that would be on her power level. No one had her kind of power. Or the power she could possess. Even casters, like her father, couldn't just disappear. They had to know the right words or ingredients to cast a spell.

Her father glared at Ainsley and ran a hand across his short, red hair. "We aren't sure. All we know is no one has seen or heard from her in three years and no locating spell has found her."

"But that doesn't mean we can't teach ye. Between your father and me, we know just as much as Meara does." Ainsley grasped Niamh's shoulder and squeezed.

Biting on the inside of her cheek, Niamh nodded. She couldn't disagree with them. She didn't know the woman they spoke of or the extent of her knowledge. Who was she to argue? "Then I guess we should get back at it."

"First, ye should go change. Those clothes hinder your initial training sessions. I picked out something that'll fit ye better." Ainsley gestured to the back bedroom.

That benefited her. Not only would she get out of the clothes clinging to her body, she'd wanted to get into that bedroom since she and Nessan arrived at the cabin earlier. It was the same one Grianne removed the tome from the day before.

Niamh stood and headed down the hall. She shut the bedroom door and glanced at the black leather pants and tan short-sleeved peasant blouse laid out atop the queen-sized bed. The clothes appeared much more appropriate. She wasn't even five-foot-tall yet and tended toward smaller sizes because of her slight frame. Before she changed into them, she shifted her gaze to the chest against the wall to her right.

Although her conversation with Grianne had shed some light on the shadows surrounding her family, she could see something was still being left out. Maybe one book in the chest could tell her what. Niamh crossed the room and lifted the lid as quietly as possible.

She didn't have a lot of time, so she'd have to skim through a few of the books quickly. She picked up a dark blue one. The cover wasn't labeled, so she flipped it open to the front page. *History of the O'Callaghan Family*. No. She selected another book. *Foliage of An Talamh Beo*. No. She chose another.

*Property of Quinlan O'Callaghan.*

Rolling over to her side, Niamh stared at the alder tree outside her bedroom window. She should sleep, but no matter how hard she tried, slumber refused to greet her. Which was surprising, given her physical exhaustion.

Bygleswurth sauntered up the blanket. A paw gently nudged at her shoulder. "Niamh, wake up."

Her catalync wasn't a tool. He had to know well she wasn't asleep. "I'm awake."

"Oh. Then, perhaps, you wish to discuss why you are tossing and turning." He lay down and draped one paw over the other.

*Not really.* The last thing she wanted to do was talk about the journal she'd found and snuck back home. It hadn't been what she'd been searching for, but it had piqued her curiosity. At first, she hadn't been able to tell which Quinlan it belonged to. It was a popular name in her family, given their tradition. With no other alternative, she skimmed the first couple of pages. It didn't take long for her to recognize the hand-writing.

It belonged to her father.

Somewhere after setting it down on the bed and changing clothes, she'd wrapped it in a thin cloth and tucked it in the back of her pants, where it remained until she and her father arrived home. Now that she had it, should she keep reading it?

The first couple of pages had spoken about his time training with Meara. He'd described her as a bit of a hard arse and complained about how much of their ancestral knowledge she'd shoved down his throat. It had been kind of amusing. At least until she read the top of the next page, which was where she had stopped. She still recalled the first line.

*I had a nightmare.*

Part of her wanted to read more; the other part warned her against further invading his privacy. How would she feel if her father read her journal? Where she described every part of the nightmare she had experienced. The one where she jotted down her research on the meanings. The one where she expressed her concerns.

"Well, if you do not wish to discuss whatever is on your mind, then may we return to sleep? You have a big day tomorrow." Bygleswurth stood and padded his way back down to the end of the bed.

She watched as her catalync curled up once again. Her father's words from earlier echoed in her brain: *It's his job to help direct ye and point ye in the right direction.* Bygleswurth was her guide. Maybe that applied to all things.

Niamh sat up. "I was going through a chest at the cabin and I found my father's journal."

Bygleswurth lifted his head. "I cannot imagine that is the issue that has plagued you all evening."

"No. I read a couple of his entries an' the last one..." Niamh paused. Biting on the inside of her cheek, she dropped her gaze and tightened her hold on the blanket. It was harder to admit than she thought possible. She had to talk to someone about her reservation. "The top of the entry referenced a nightmare. I didn't keep reading, but I feel like I should."

"I am going to ignore the blatant violation of privacy. I am presuming you wish to continue reading about his nightmare in the hopes it might provide some insight into your own."

Niamh canted her head. She wouldn't have put it quite like that, but he had summed up her anxiety over the situation rather well.

"Yeah. If he experienced 'em when he was younger, maybe it relates to mine." And maybe their nightmares together could explain the shadows. Or even lead her to identify the darkness hunting her family. There were several ways she believed it could be helpful. That was the problem.

"While I understand your turmoil, perhaps instead of reading his words, take this opportunity to talk to Quinlan about your dreams."

She opened her mouth and snapped it shut. Her father hadn't been the most forthcoming person over the past couple of days. Even if she confronted him about the nightmares, what would prevent him from dodging her questions or offering half-answers? Something he had gotten extremely good at. Niamh fidgeted with the starry, midnight blue comforter over her legs. "Do ye think he'd actually tell me about it?"

"I believe if you offered him information about your own, he would share his."

Narrowing her eyes, she studied Bygleswurth. It wasn't shocking to realize he had an aura, too. She had discovered a lot of creatures and any yoke, including trees and rocks, had auras. Not everything was inanimate, as she had grown to believe. In his, she saw a lot of bright yellow. "You know something about 'is nightmares, don't ye?"

Bygleswurth sighed. "I do not know the details, only that it was a vision, like yours, of something dark coming."

She threw the covers aside, hopped out of bed, and went straight for her nightstand.

"Niamh, no!" He jumped down and landed right in front of the nightstand.

"Get out of my way."

Why hadn't she seen it before? She should've read the entire entry back at the cabin. Then she wouldn't be here arguing with her catalync over the key to saving her family.

"I cannot do that. I cannot allow you to entrench your father's privacy."

"Ye don't have a choice. I'm not going to let the darkness steal my family. I know his vision will tell me what I need to know about the shadows. So, move or I'll move ye." Niamh held her hand out and tried calling the current she'd successfully used at least twice. After the thing with her cousin yesterday, she realized her powers were linked to her emotions. Her hand sparked.

"Shadows? Did you say shadows?"

"Yes. My family has been marked—"

"For death." As soon as the words left his maw, Bygleswurth stepped aside.

The spark in her hand fizzled. Niamh stared at her catalync and swallowed some saliva to wet her dry throat. Everyone around her understood what it meant, and she truly hated it. She was grateful they did, but it felt like she had taken the longest route possible to get to the truth.

Inhaling deeply, she opened the top drawer of her nightstand, but only her journal laid there. She lifted her journal and searched underneath it. Nothing. She could've sworn she had left it in the top drawer. Thinking back, she retraced her steps.

As soon as she and her father walked into the house, she had raced up the staircase, come straight into her room and tucked her father's journal neatly in the drawer. Niamh yanked open the second and third drawer, but the journal wasn't in either of them.

"Is something wrong?"

"It's gone. The journal's gone." There was no other choice. She'd have to talk to her father now.

Quinlan brushed a low-hanging tree branch aside. Was this the right part of Barna Woods? He'd gotten what details he could from Nessan last night without giving his thoughts away. While he didn't believe shadows appeared or that a soul-snatcher developed, he had to check things out for himself. If for no other reason than to prove his cousin wrong. Even though it meant he'd lied to his wife regarding his whereabouts.

After he'd spotted his daughter yesterday with one of his journals, the less his family knew, the better off they all were. His cousin could handle her training for one day without him. He wrinkled his nose as the wind carried a horrid scent in the air. Di'Lacia that was something awful. It smelled like a combination of rotten fish and ... sulfur.

That wasn't good. It couldn't be the rise of a soul-snatcher. Many creatures carried that kind of stench. The smell of fire and brimstone. The wind shuddered through the branches as he followed the foul odor of decay. He trekked past a small gathering of tall trees when he spotted a group of fallen trees leaning drunkenly against one another. Each charred in multiple places.

It looked like the remnants of a battle, except with no bodies. He stepped over broken branches and dead leaves, searching for a clue to what had happened. The hair on the back of his neck stood on end. Quinlan placed a hand on the hilt of his sword.

He wasn't alone.

Stopping in front of a tree, he skimmed his fingertips across the rough, cracked ridges of tree bark. It was sticky and black. As he yanked his blade free from its scabbard, he spun around and came face-to-face with a shadow. A creature that was nothing more than black goo with a humanoid shape, but no face. It screeched as he swung his sword at it.

The creature dodged his attack. "You are not ours to kill," it hissed.

Quinlan lunged forward, and the shadow disappeared. "What the feck?" He searched his surroundings, yet saw nothing except for the rotten trees he'd seen on his arrival. Where the fuck had it gone? What did it mean? Shadows killed. It was that simple. But if they couldn't kill him … then that meant … his nightmare.

"Dava!" He took off and ran through the woods toward his truck. *Di'Lacia, please let me get to her in time.*

Niamh pursed her lips. Her cousins had moved into the last slate of her training—her power. Everything she'd done yesterday didn't compare to how hard she worked today. They'd already been at this for hours with sword exercises and archery. Who knew there were so many ways to deflect a sword attack? Or that her biceps could burn in agony? Ainsley refused to let her stop shooting until she'd gotten at least two bulls' eyes in a row. That had taken a few hours. How long would it take to control even a portion of her power?

"Obviously, ye have figured out your power and emotions are connected. The key is learning how to harness that." Ainsley pulled her hair down, raked her fingers through it, and twisted it into a bun.

"How am I s'posed to do that?" Niamh stared at the wooden man in front of her. Was she supposed to get upset with a target made of birch? Or annoyed with it somehow?

"Focus on your feelings. The stronger your focus gets, the more powerful your electroshock will be."

She cocked an eyebrow. Her what? "What is an electroshock?"

"The electricity that flows o'er your body. That is an electroshock. It's your second power. Ye get more as your power grows. Now, stop asking questions and give it a go."

Right. Focus on her emotions. Hmm, what should she focus on? That she was tired. Or the journal that someone had stolen from her bedroom. Or the frustration she had with her father, as he had yet to show up. How could she talk to him about his nightmare if he worked all day? Yeah, she got it; pub business had to be dealt with, but she needed him too. She needed him here.

Her hand sparked.

Niamh eyed Ainsley and grinned.

"Good, now keep going."

*Keep going.* Right. What had she been thinking about? Oh yeah, her father's current lack of involvement. Though he was working to take care of their family and he had always been there for her. At no point had he really let her down. The current covering her hand waned. "Shit! I lost it."

"I'm not gonna scold you about your language, but best ye not use it around your father. Try again."

Holding her hand out in front of her body, she refocused on her emotions. What else did she have to go on? The issues she had with her father no longer existed. Her gowl of a brother had probably stolen her father's journal thinking it was hers. And her exhaustion didn't help anyone.

"Come on; stop acting a maggot an' focus."

She wasn't being foolish. Niamh glared at Ainsley. "I'm trying."

"Try harder."

What other emotions did she have? Aside from the annoyance of her cousin at the moment. Not that it would—current sparked to life all over her hand and then dissipated.

"I'm thinking ye really are wee."

Gads, she loathed that word. It was the worst word in the world. No one should ever be called small or tiny or short. She wasn't any of them. Her whole body shook and electricity flickered to life all around her. With a scowl, Niamh held her hand out toward a tree in her cousin's backyard and a bolt of lightning struck it.

Ainsley clapped. "About time."

She peered over her shoulder at her cousin and regarded the tree. The tree hadn't done anything to her, but she had used her magick on it. Niamh sighed. "I'm proud and upset at the same time."

"Ye should be proud," Nessan commented from the chair he occupied. "You keep this up, an' you can deal with the mess we have brewing in Barna Woods."

"What mess?" No one had mentioned anything about a problem. Was it something she had to face? Training was important, but going right into things might be better.

"It's nothing ye need to worry over," Ainsley declared.

Why did they do that? Yesterday, they all agreed she was special. Unlike any other guardhian. Yet, today it was as if none of that happened. "Please don't treat me like a wee one. I'm the guardhian an' if there's a problem I need to address, then I need to know."

"Your father—"

"Isn't here," Niamh finished for Ainsley. "I decide what I should know." This was her realm, her responsibility. It was time they all acted like it. She turned her attention to Nessan. "What's the mess?"

"I've seen shadows there. I don't know if you've read about them, but they're dangerous creatures. They consume energy. At least one shapeshifter has died from an attack. Another is on the brink of death," Nessan reported. "You're the only one that can kill 'em. At least two wanders 'bout the woods."

It wasn't something she'd read about yet, but they sounded bad. The hairs on her arms stood at attention. Niamh scoured her surroundings. The tree she'd destroyed remained in place. As did the wooden practice dummy she used for training. Nessan and Bygleswurth still occupied the back porch. Ainsley stood beside her. Nothing about the backyard appeared off.

But something dark was nearby.

Really dark.

Her eyes widened. Niamh darted out the gate and ran as hard as her feet would carry her to her house. She heard Ainsley, Nessan, and Bygleswurth call after her, but she didn't have time to explain.

There was no time to stop.

The heels of her boots pounded against the dirt road as she raced for her house. It had come. She didn't know what she would face when she got there, but she had training. No matter how little she had received, she would do whatever it took to protect her family.

She dashed up the porch steps and barged into the house through the back door. The kitchen was empty, save for the smell of baked beef. The mixed sweet scent of thyme, tomato paste, and Worcestershire sauce hit her nostrils. Her mother had been making dinner.

The darkness was there. She could sense it.

Niamh unsheathed the sword at her hip and she proceeded forward to the dining room. Her mother had propped the swinging doors open. Something the female liked to do when she was back and forth between the kitchen and upstairs. But where were all the lights? They were all turned off, which was weird.

From the middle of the dining room, she scanned the hallway. Nothing stood out to her, but she could feel it. Whatever *it* was, was close by. Cautiously, Niamh slipped through the doorway and into the hall.

Out of her periphery, she saw something spring into action. It knocked her down. She lost her hold on her sword, and it went skittering across the floor. Twisting onto her side, Niamh swung her forearm up and hit its maw with the gauntlet she had on.

That didn't stop it for long. It lunged at her.

She used her forearm to dodge its teeth from sinking into her neck.

It clamped its teeth around her forearm.

The gauntlet protected her a little, but it wouldn't last forever. This was the first chance she had to get a look at her opponent. It was a black wolf. Not just its fur, but its eyes too. Actually, everything about it was black, even its aura.

Almost as if it didn't have one.

Or didn't have a soul.

The wolf's teeth broke through the leather gauntlet and pierced her skin.

She howled out in pain. Her dagger was out of reach. She couldn't get to the bow on her back. Feck. It pushed against her arm, almost as if it was trying to break it. She had to do something. Niamh concentrated on the agony coursing through her body. Using that and combining it with her fear, she called an electroshock all over her body and electrocuted the wolf.

It flew into the wall and landed on the ground with a massive thud.

Panting heavily, she scrambled to her feet and snagged her sword. Holding the blade up with one clammy hand, she clutched her other arm to her body. Her stomach flip-flopped as she eyeballed the wolf on the floor. Its fur was truly all black. And it was bigger than she expected. Almost the size of a shapeshifter. Which was certainly strange enough, as all black wolves were extinct, but the aura on this creature was the weirdest part.

There wasn't one.

The black she had previously seen before had disappeared, or maybe it never existed.

Unless she had killed it.

The latter was the most logical. No way any creature survived the electroshock she'd generated.

Right?

Bile rose up the back of her throat. She swallowed and inhaled a deep breath to keep from throwing up. Di'Lacia she shouldn't be bothered by its death; it had been there to kill her family. Niamh glanced toward the staircase.

Where were her parents? With all the noise, she presumed they'd come down the stairs. Or at least to the top of the staircase. Maybe they were still hiding. Before she searched for her parents, she needed to check on the wolf. Gradually, she inched toward the creature. Once she was close enough, she nudged it with the tip of her sword.

It didn't budge.

Looked like it really was dead. Now, she just had to go find her parents and let them know it was safe. Blood trickled down her forearm. Niamh kept the blade in front of her body and ambled up the stairs. Nothing came at her. Nothing jumped out from the hallway upstairs. She poked her head in her bedroom. It was exactly as she had left it this morning.

Niamh strode across the hall to her brother's bedroom. She nudged his door. It swung open with a slight creak. Only his furniture and *The Godfather* and *The Godfather Part II* posters greeted her. He wasn't anywhere to be seen.

Slowly, she made her way to her parents' bedroom.

It was too quiet.

"Mum? Daidí?" She called out as she opened their door.

The sword fell from her hand, clattering to the floor. There was blood everywhere. It covered the walls and her parents' bed. "Mum!" Niamh rushed across the threshold to her mother's side. Her mother lay across the bed with a deep gash across her throat. She wasn't breathing or even gasping for air, and her aura had completely vanished. Still, she covered her mother's neck to stop the bleeding. "Mum!"

Tears rolled down her cheeks. "No, no, no," Niamh muttered. She needed a towel. Where was a towel? She had to stop the bleeding. Her mother was losing too much. There had to be a towel ... or something she could use. Niamh stood to run to the attached bathroom and froze. Her pulse quickened, her eyes widened, and she trembled. Oh gods, this couldn't be happening.

"Daidí?" she croaked out. Her father lay on the ground in a heap. There was more blood on the surrounding walls. A pool of crimson covered the floor. Like her mother, he wasn't struggling for air and he had no aura.

All she could sense was the anger and pain and fear that lingered. As if someone had betrayed their family. Turned against the love they all had for one another. The entire room went still.

Something snapped her back to the present. She ran to her father and rolled him over. He had several smaller gashes than her mother. His throat ... "Please, no," Niamh mumbled. Grabbing a piece of clothing or towel off the floor somewhere, she pressed it against the gaping hole in his neck. *Please, let him be alive. Please, let him be alive.* Niamh leaned down and listened for a heartbeat. Nothing. She heard nothing. Sitting back up, she positioned one hand over his heart and placed the heel of her palm atop of it. She pressed her hands down the way they had learned in school and tried to get his heart beating. "Come on. Come on."

Her vision blurred. Tears streamed down her face. Not that she cared. She couldn't stop. After all the fighting and pushing for her training, things couldn't end like this. She inclined her head to his heart and listened again. Still nothing. There hadn't been anything for her to find.

The creature hadn't been coming to kill her parents; it had already succeeded. Her heart shattered in front of her eyes. "No, no, no, no, no, no, no."

This couldn't be happening. She couldn't fail them like this. Not when they'd all finally gotten on the same page. Not when she'd gained a sliver of momentum with her powers. It couldn't end this way. "Daidí, please," Niamh whispered through her tears. "Please, don't leave me. Please," she pleaded.

There was no response. Only silence greeted her. Her parents would never utter another word to her again.

Her father was gone.

Her mother was gone.

There was nothing she could do to save them. Niamh sobbed. Her entire body shook. Electricity surged through her veins.

How had she failed? How had she missed the signs? She had fought that creature and it still stole them from her. If only she'd gotten there sooner, or trusted her gut more, then she could've protected them.

This shouldn't have happened.

Except it had.

They were gone. And she'd never get them back.

"NOOOOO!" Niamh wailed.

Voltage exploded from her body. Lightning shot from her fingertips. It struck the curtains in her parents' bedroom and sparked a fire. The current expelled from her body in multiple directions. The entire house lit up like fireworks on Saint Patrick's Day.

Her spirit settled, and she collapsed.

# CHAPTER EIGHT

Niamh groaned. There was something damp against her forehead. And her forearm throbbed. Had it gotten rough in training? She couldn't remember. Why couldn't she—

*My parents.* She bolted upright and blinked. This wasn't her bedroom. This wasn't her parents' bedroom. She was in the cabin. The same back bedroom she had been in multiple times before. Maybe this had all been a nightmare. Niamh picked up the wet washcloth from her lap. It must've fallen. She eyed the bandage around her forearm.

Had she hurt herself in training? No. That wasn't what happened. She swallowed the tears threatening to spill over. *Please, please, let this be a bad dream.* Unhurriedly, she got to her feet and climbed out of the bed.

"You are awake. Ainsley, Grianne, Nessan, she is awake." Bygleswurth trotted across the room and hopped up on the bed. "We were so worried about you."

Her eyebrows furrowed and her gaze dropped to the floor as she sat back down. She was afraid to ask, but she had to know. Nightmare or reality? "What ... what happened?"

"I found you in the upstairs bedroom ... passed out." Bygleswurth's eyes softened, and he sat down beside her.

So, it was true. She had failed her parents. Silently, Niamh wept.

Ainsley stepped through the door first. She bolted across the room and wrapped her arms around Niamh. Nessan hugged her next. Grianne embraced her last.

All she could do was sit there, unmoving. They were all grateful she'd survived. It would've been better if she had died in that house.

With her family.

Her family. Niamh gasped and snapped her attention back to Bygleswurth. "What about my brother? Did anyone find him?"

Nessan shook his head. "We only found ye with your parents. The rest of the house was empty."

"What of the black wolf?" She had killed him. She had checked. He'd been down on the ground. He hadn't moved.

"There was no creature anywhere when I found you upstairs. After that, we were more concerned with your safe retrieval before the fire consumed the house," Bygleswurth said.

She studied each of them, one by one. Every word they uttered had been truthful. Not a single lie amongst the group. Not only had she failed to protect her parents, she had also failed to kill their murderer. She had to go back to the house and search for clues as to the identity of that black wolf. Deep in her soul, she knew he alone was responsible for the death of her parents. Niamh stood. "I need to go back."

Nessan, Bgyleswurth, and Grianne all turned to Ainsley.

Ainsley gripped the back of her neck. "I'm afraid that isn't a possibility. The fire brigade did all they could to put out the blaze, but there wasn't much left by the time they did. Last I checked, the shades were still investigatin' to determine a cause of the fire."

"I suspect your police will not conclude more than lightning; however, it does not make it safe to return," Bygleswurth added on.

She couldn't believe she was hearing this. It was bad enough her parents were gone, but she couldn't even seek the one who took them and exact revenge?

It wasn't fair.

It wasn't right.

They shouldn't be gone.

Her parents shouldn't be dead.

Her lips trembled. She wrapped her arms around her stomach. Her entire body ached. It felt as if someone had taken a hammer to her heart, belly, and every muscle all at the same time. Every part of her was being pulled apart piece by piece by piece.

And she couldn't stop it.

Tears rolled down her cheeks, and she fell to her knees. Sparks lit up her fingertips, elbows, and ears. Burying her face in her hands, Niamh bawled.

Grianne kneeled down beside her and cradled her against her chest. She enfolded her wings around her, simply holding her tight.

Niamh stared at the door to her father's pub. According to her cousins, her brother had spent most of the last few days there. Not that she knew why. He always hated the pub. Her brother would only go when forced.

It had been three days since her parents' death. Three days of endless tears. Niamh had spent most of her time in bed in the back bedroom of the cabin. She hadn't had the desire to go out, even to search for her brother. Instead, Nessan and Ainsley had done that on her behalf.

And they'd found him.

Alive and well.

The news should've thrilled her, but it didn't. Where had he been when that wolf had attacked their parents? He could've helped save them. Stopped the creature that took them away. She'd been stupid to think she could do it all on her own. Her parents paid for her mistake. She couldn't blame her brother for that, which was why she stood there, ready to face him.

"Ye don't have to go in, ye know?" Nessan said.

"I have to go, but I appreciate it." She had to check on her brother and see how he was fairing through this tragedy.

Nessan nodded. "I'll be out here when you're ready to leave."

"Thank ye." Niamh brushed her fingers through her hair and wiped the unshed tears from the corners of her eyes. Inhaling and exhaling deeply, she mustered up the strength to go inside. The pub was bustling with men toting boxes full of pictures her father had hung on the wall. Several people she didn't know cleaned.

Her eyes tracked the movement of two of the men. What were they doing with her father's things? Where were they taking it all? Niamh started after them.

Quinlan, her brother, stepped into her path. "Where have you been? I was worried ye got caught in the fire, too."

Gads. Some awful smell permeated her nostrils. Covering her nose and mouth, Niamh eyed her brother. He had changed. His hair was darker, almost a midnight black. And his aura was the same way. Had something significant changed with him? No. She refused to think like that. This was her brother. It had to be the grief weighing on him. Just like it weighed on her. Niamh inched back further and removed her hand from her face. A bit of distance helped her tolerate the stench. "I'm sorry, but ye smell rotten."

"It's probably from workin' in here. I've been sweatin' a bit."

This wasn't any kind of sweat stench she'd ever caught a whiff of; it was like rancid fish. Maybe he'd been working in the dumpster out back. Not that it explained the other changes. She shook her head and thought back to her original explanation. Grief. "Where are they takin' Daidí's things?"

"We've been getting the pub ready for the new owner."

Her eyes widened, and her jaw dropped open. "New owner? We can't let someone take Daidí's pub. He loved this place. And it's all we have left."

"There isn't much we can do. Daidí sold it a few days ago."

A few days ago? Had her father prepared for his death? But how ... Niamh blinked. Could it have been the nightmare he had? The one she didn't read or talk to him about? That couldn't be right. No way would her father leave her like this. She had to believe he would've done everything in his power to stay here with her.

Their deaths were on her. The only other one she blamed was the wolf. That wasn't entirely true. There was another.

"Have ye told her?"

The voice snapped her out of her reverie. Her eyes landed on the stubby nose and bloated cheeks that went with it. She clenched her fists up and narrowed her eyes. He was the other person she placed at fault.

Séamus.

"Not yet," Quinlan said.

"Tell me what?" Niamh uttered through gritted teeth.

"You'll be staying with me." Séamus grinned.

"What?" That made no sense. She and her brother had relatives here. And this man, who was no doubt a chancer, definitely wasn't on that list. He had only been her father's boss. Nothing more.

Her brother nodded. "It's what our parents wanted."

"I don't understand. Why wouldn't we stay with Ainsley? She's family." That was exactly where they should be in this time of loss; with family. Not to mention she had a lot of training to undergo. That wolf may have escaped once, but he sure as hell wouldn't get away a second time.

She would find him.

And avenge her parents.

"You can't always trust family," Séamus replied.

He had to be kidding. To her, they were way more loyal than him. Niamh swallowed the bile threatening to claw up the back of her throat. She couldn't come out and say that, though. She was thirteen. Her rights were limited. Maybe she could plead her case ... to her brother. He would be in charge, sort of. Softening her gaze, she looked to Quinlan. "I'd feel more comfortable staying with Ainsley and Nessan."

"We'll discuss this tomorrow after the wake. For now, we'll stay with Séamus." Her brother reached out and squeezed her shoulder.

She shrugged, free of his grasp. His touch made her skin crawl. Grief or not, something had happened to him. Her brother had changed. "Tomorrow? Don't ye think it's soon? I'm sure Ainsley—"

"Enough with our cousins!" Pinching the bridge of his nose, Quinlan rubbed the back of his head and sighed. "Séamus has already planned everything. The wake is being held at his house, where we will be staying. Ye don't want their spirits to get stuck 'ere, now do ye?"

"Absolutely not, but I'm not spending the night in a strange house with a man I don't know!" How dare he try to use that against her? Niamh spun on the heel of her sneaker and stomped out the door.

"Is everything—"

Her brother interrupted Nessan's question and grabbed her arm. "Where do ye think you're going?"

Niamh yanked her arm free. She opened her mouth, but didn't get very far. Narrowing his eyes, Nessan stepped beside her and nudged her behind him. She half-complied and stood at an angle to her cousin's back. Either way, he was between her and her brother. As for her brother, where she planned to go was back to the cabin. It was a hell of a lot safer than where she was right now, but she didn't intend to tell him that. "I'm staying the night with Ainsley and Nessan. Do ye have a problem with that?"

Crossing his arms, Quinlan frowned. "Not at all, but I expect to see ye at the wake tomorrow. I'll pick ye up around noon."

"I'll be ready." With that, she and her cousin walked over to the truck they'd ridden to the pub in and left.

Niamh brushed aside another spiderweb. Gads, how many of these things could one forest contain? After the situation with her brother, Nessan convinced her and Ainsley to make a trip to Barna Woods. Focusing on a mission kept her mind off of the shitshow that had become her life. "Are ye sure we're goin' in the right direction?"

"I am. I fought against the shadows. So, I know exactly where I saw them," Nessan responded.

"I believe you, but I thought they gave off a stench." At least, according to her research, they smelled like fire. Niamh blinked. An image of the yellow curtains in her parents' bedroom flashed before her eyes. Flames licked at the bottom, crawling toward the top. She shook her head, and a rotten log a couple of feet in front of her replaced the vision. Sweat bloomed across her palm as she tightened the grip she had on the hilt of her sword.

"... don't know why we haven't picked up the scent," Nessan stated. "I swear we're close." He pointed at a pair of crisscrossed trees. "Those are familiar."

"Then maybe we'll find their lair soon." Whatever he'd said prior that didn't seem all that important. That wasn't true. She just couldn't let this tragedy take control of her life. Nothing could be changed. The sooner she accepted that, the sooner ... feck. She didn't know.

"There." Her cousin gestured to a group of charred fallen trees. "That's where I found the shapeshifter."

Obviously, someone had moved his body, which didn't surprise her. Shapeshifter customs aligned with their own for their dead. As they got closer, Niamh sniffed the air. Still nothing. It smelled musty, but that was it. She glanced at her cousins. "I'm not gettin' anything."

"Neither am I." Nessan groaned and shoved a hand through his hair. "I don't understand. Shadows don't just up and disappear, do they?"

"Not that I know of," Ainsley replied. "Let's take some samples from the trees. We can analyze them back at the cabin later."

Damn. She'd really needed to kill something. As there wasn't anything to fight, there was little she could do. "I agree." They could always come back another day. "In the meantime, ye should let the alpha know. It might be best if he continues patrols until we find these things."

"Though he probably won't like it, I'll tell 'im. As long as he knows we aren't givin' up, I'm sure he'll see it as what's best."

They weren't giving up. Those words weren't in her vocabulary. Just like she planned to find that black wolf one day, she'd find these shadows and destroy them. "Never give up," Niamh repeated.

Niamh stared at herself in the mirror. The fire destroyed most of her clothes. The only clothes she had were whatever she found inside the chests at the cabin. In one bedroom, she had located a suitable dress, but it certainly wouldn't have been her first choice.

The dress was emerald green; it matched the color of her eyes. It was tea-length with an A-line cut; whatever that meant. Looking at her reflection, the dress hovered just above her knee. The top half was sleeveless and covered in green flowers. A satin belt wrapped around her waist with a bow in the front. The inside skirting was also satin and draped in tulle.

It was a beautiful dress, and it suited her perfectly. It fit the same way too; almost as if it had been specifically chosen for her. Bright colors were the tradition at a wake, but she felt like she'd stand out in this contraption.

"I still don't like this," Nessan said from the doorway.

"Ye and Ainsley will both be there, so it'll be fine." At least at the wake. She hadn't quite figured out how to get out of staying with Séamus.

"I'm talking 'bout after the wake. You still need to train, and I can't protect ye if I can't even get in to see ye."

Sighing, she brushed the skirting of the dress down one last time and walked over to the bed she'd slept in the night before. They had returned to her cousin's house last night in case her brother unexpectedly dropped by for a visit. But a necessary one. She had left Bygleswurth with Grianne back at the cabin.

Whatever she'd seen in her brother yesterday, Nessan had noticed it too.

She still chalked it up to grief. Niamh snagged the matching shoes that had been in the chest with the dress and slipped her feet into the flats. "I'm good at sneaking out. Besides, I'd like to know if some sickness has taken over my brother."

"What if he is sick? What's stopping it from coming after you?"

"I don't know, but I have to do something. The darkness may not have gotten to 'im yet." She had seen the shadow on him at one point. It was no longer with her brother from what she gathered, but something had taken its place.

Nessan shoved his hands in the pockets of his periwinkle slacks. "Maybe I can talk to Quinlan. Convince him to an arrangement that will appeal to his senses."

"Without fighting him?" She raised an eyebrow. Yesterday, outside the pub, her cousin and brother had thrown off so much tension. For a minute, she believed they would get into a fight.

"I promise not to hit him ... unless he throws the first punch."

"There will be no brawling," Ainsley said. "We may not trust the man holding the wake, but it is for our family. Ye will be respectful of that."

Her cousin had a point. This was for her parents. That mattered. Not who had set up the celebration of their lives. Tears welled in the corners of her eyes and rolled down her cheeks. A knock at the front door pulled her out of her despair. It had to be her brother. Sniffling, Niamh wiped away the tears and collected herself.

Niamh stared at the orange SUV in the parking lot of her father's pub. The excessive number of auras overwhelmed her, so she'd slipped away from the wake. Her absence had probably gone unnoticed. She didn't know most of the attendees. They only seemed to have known her father. She had to go some place where she'd be comfortable.

When she had first arrived at the house, she hadn't been positive sneaking off the property would even be possible. Turned out to be easier than she expected. There had been a hidden gate in the garden, past the pond and just beyond the fountain. Man, she was grateful for that.

Although, if she hadn't suggested to Nessan, they meet back up at the cabin in an hour and a half, she would've never escaped alone. It was a personal request. Niamh readjusted the strap over her shoulder and patted the bag at her side.

She shifted her gaze from the SUV to the butterfly-wind-chime hanging by the front door of the pub. Her father had carved and hollowed each chime by hand. It had been so a key would easily fit inside. She stroked the smoothness of each chime. On the last one, she removed the hidden key, unlocked the pub and let herself in.

Yeah, the new owner was apparently there, but she didn't care. She needed to be close to her father for a bit, and this was the best place for it. Niamh walked over to one of the high-top tables and ran her hand across the polished wood. This past year, she and her father had sanded a few of the tabletops and stained them together.

The door to the backroom opened and a slightly older woman, close to her mother's age, stepped out carrying a box in her arms. She trekked over to the bar, set the box down and cocked an eyebrow. "Can I help ye?"

"I'm sorry. I didn't mean to let myself in." That wasn't true. She had intentionally sought the hidden key, but she shouldn't have. Niamh frowned. She turned around and headed for the front door.

"Wait, a second. Are ye Niamh?"

She stopped with her hand on the doorknob and blinked. The woman knew her name. How? Slowly, Niamh pivoted on the ball of her foot. "Have we met?"

"Oh, no. I've only ever seen pictures of you. Your father showed me."

"Ye knew my father?" Her nose crinkled. How was that possible? She swore she knew all of his friends. Then again; her mind wandered back to the group of people she'd left behind at the wake. That didn't even include everything about the realm she hadn't known about until a week ago.

"Your father and I grew up together. I'm Rhea." The red-headed woman extended her hand.

Hesitantly, Niamh shook her hand and studied the woman. Not just her physical appearance, but her aura as well. What kind of person was she? Rhea had short, auburn red hair and honey-colored eyes. She was tall for a woman, somewhere around five foot eleven, give or take an inch. She was also rather muscular. The clear metallic gold in her aura explained that, though.

Niamh canted her head. "You're a shapeshifter."

"I am." Rhea narrowed her eyes and furrowed her brows. "It's true, then? You have … a third eye?"

She readjusted the bag over her shoulder again and dropped her gaze to the floor. Maybe she shouldn't have come right out and stated what she noticed about Rhea's aura, but part of her hoped this woman would become an ally. It was too late to take the words back now. Niamh bit the inside of her cheek and nodded. "I s'pose ye could say that."

Crossing her arms, Rhea sighed. "Your father didn't tell you about me, did he?"

"No. I didn't even know he'd sold the pub until my brother told me yesterday." It seemed normal to know practically nothing regarding her father. He likely had his reasons, but it would be nice to understand them.

"I'd kick his arse if he wasn't already gone." Rhea gestured to a booth. "Why don't we sit an' talk for a moment?"

Niamh glanced at the booth. She didn't know how long she'd been here already. It would take time for her to get back to the cabin, although she hadn't really thought about how she planned to get there either. She still had the dress on and hitch-hiking wasn't recommended. Surely, she could spare a few minutes while she figured out her transportation.

The two of them crossed the pub and sat opposite one another in one of the wooden booths. Rhea steepled her fingers together. "Your father knew his time left was short. I don't know the details, so don't ask. All I know is he prepared for it by signing the pub over to me and setting up a few clauses in the contract that would ensure I looked after you."

Niamh opened her mouth and snapped it shut. She had presumed her father had known something was hunting him and her mother because of his nightmare, but this had been the first actual confirmation she had. Based on what Bygleswurth had told her, she suspected Grianne knew the details, but with his passing ... she didn't want to know. At least not yet.

As for this woman looking out for her ... how did he expect her to do that when she would live with a horrible man? She was so confused. "I don't understand. How?"

"Well, according to the contract, I get you as an employee. His intention is that while ye will spend some time working 'ere, it will also serve as a cover for your training."

"Did he explain why?" The question popped out of her mouth before she stopped it. With her and her brother having to live with Séamus, it made sense for her to require a cover, but it wouldn't have even been necessary if their living arrangements had been different.

"The only thing he said was that he had gotten backed into a corner and this was his only way out."

Hanging her head, Niamh groaned. Her father, a man full of secrets. This was great. Every conversation she had with someone who truly knew her father left her with more and more questions. "How much did he tell ye about me?"

"He told me you have abilities, and that there is a realm 'ere that you're responsible for guarding."

Niamh lifted her head. She may have very well just found her ride. She was tired of secrets and got the sense this woman wouldn't just be an ally, but a friend. "Would ye be okay goin' somewhere with me?"

"I'd be all right with that."

"Grand." It wasn't the same as having her father by her side, but at least she'd have someone on the outside to talk to about stuff. Someone who could offer a different perspective. Maybe that's what her father believed she'd need through all of this.

Apparently, escorting new people to the realm was forbidden. All of them, her cousins, Bygleswurth, and Grianne, yelled at her about bringing Rhea into *An Talamh Beo*. Niamh had responded by telling them to lighten up and trust her judgment.

To prove she was safe, Rhea had shifted to her animal form. Since the woman didn't have any spare clothes, she had gone behind a tree to transform. It would've been interesting to see if she changed any differently than her brother or Nessan, aside from her animal form.

Rhea was a fox. A red fox, to be exact. The auburn red hair and amber eyes should've been a dead giveaway, but Niamh hadn't really put two and two together.

After that, everyone seemed satisfied Rhea was one of the good guys. Which was grand, given the journey they were undertaking.

Niamh had switched out her clothes for something more appropriate to the land. Her boots, black leather pants, tan peasant blouse, and a green jacket she'd discovered amidst the chests. She had loaded up with her weapons and led the way.

Nessan had offered to carry Bygleswurth, while she carried ... her parents. Before she had snuck away from the wake, she'd come across the room that contained her parents' remains. Although someone had turned all the mirrors around and the window in the room had been open, the room had also been empty.

All that remained of her parents were ashes, but she fully intended for their spirits to be at peace. They deserved that. So, with a little help from Nessan, she switched out the urns.

The six of them trekked through the forest with her in front. She didn't know the layout of the land, but she had learned to trust her instincts a bit more. That was precisely what she followed.

As her ears perked up, Niamh slowed her pace. Not far off, she could hear the water gushing over the rocks. The waterfall would be a perfect place to release her parents' ashes.

They hiked for a little while longer and finally approached the waterfall. It was absolutely exquisite. It resembled a wall of crystal-blue ribbon glistening under the full moon. The water swished over the rocks and thundered down the mountainside. Niamh stood there and drank it all in. "This is where they should be laid to rest."

"Are ye sure?" Nessan asked as he lifted Bygleswurth off his shoulder.

Grianne spread her wings. A gentle breeze ruffled her feathers. "They will be at peace here."

"This is amazing." Rhea stepped up beside Niamh.

None of the last week had been easy for her, but she kept pushing forward. And she would continue to do so, no matter what life sent her way. Carefully, she set the bag down and eyed the two urns. She wanted to release them simultaneously, but she couldn't do it alone.

Niamh glanced over at the group. Bygleswurth was obviously out since he stood on four paws. Grianne would be a good choice, but she wasn't certain how it would impact her purity. Ainsley or Rhea were another great option, but they weren't the best.

She shifted her eyes to Nessan. He was the closest thing she had to a brother since she didn't currently trust her own. Her cousin ... her prohtector was the best choice. "Will ye help me set them free together?"

"If that's what ye want, I can."

With a quick dip of her chin, she reached down, selected one urn, and handed it to him. Niamh reached down again and collected the second urn. She couldn't believe that the two people she had loved for the last thirteen years had been reduced to cinders. It had been at her own hand, too. She remembered discovering their bodies, and then electricity had crawled all over her and ignited a fire. Tears welled in the corners of her eyes as she struggled to control her emotions.

Her hand sparked. She swallowed the tears threatening to spill over. Niamh inhaled and exhaled deeply. She had to let them go.

Collecting herself together, she nodded to Nessan.

Together, they removed the covers and shook the ashes out until they completely emptied them. The wind billowed around them and swept the ashes away. It whisked the tiny fragments through the cascading water and up into the air.

Tears rolled down her cheeks as she watched the wind carry her parents off. One day, she would see them again.

Rhea placed a hand on Niamh's shoulder and squeezed. "Your father would be proud of how you handled this."

"Ye think so?" She wasn't positive he would have been. She had purposely left her brother out and she was more determined than ever to find her parents' killer.

"I agree," Ainsley said. "You have shown great strength these last few days."

Great strength? Niamh grimaced. She disagreed. Not that she'd openly show it. Her strength wasn't great. Not yet, but she would get there.

"Thank you, but I can be stronger. An' when I am, I'll avenge my parents' deaths."

"I know you are set on locating their murderer and while I will not fault you that, I must remind you, there are others who depend on you," Bygleswurth said.

Niamh eyeballed her catalync. She hadn't forgotten about her duties. Evidently, neither had he. The good news about all of this was she could address one while working toward the other. She had to guard the realm and all of its inhabitants, but she didn't have to forego searching for that black wolf. The realm just took a priority.

"You're right. I am a Guardhian. I am responsible for the creatures in this realm. They come first."

TO BE CONTINUED ...

KEEP READING FOR A PREVIEW OF DISILLUSIONED
BOOK TWO

Finishing the braid, Niamh stared at herself in the mirror. She looked more like her mother every day. The freckles peppered across her nose hadn't changed any in the last three years. Her hair had lightened some from all the time she'd spent out in the sun. It was closer to a fiery red than the crimson she had as a child. The rest of her body had filled out as she'd gotten older and taller.

She was now the same height as her mother had been; a solid five-foot-seven-inches.

That was where the similarities ended. Her legs, arms, and abdomen had more muscle than she ever recalled on her mother. Her father had been the one with all the muscle. It had been the physical labor he'd endured working in the pub. Not to mention the training he had gone through as a teenager.

It was the same training she'd received regularly over the last few years. Most days she spent at the cabin or at Ainsley's desperately working to improve her physical prowess and control her powers. Nearly three years and she hardly felt as if she'd learned anything at all.

Probably a good thing she hadn't found that black wolf yet.

She didn't have to focus on that today. She had work at the pub this evening. Niamh inhaled a deep breath and eyed the reflection of the green t-shirt Rhea had elected for the employees to wear a couple of years ago. She hated it, but only because it made her emerald green eyes stand out more. If she could've changed her eye color, she would, except she didn't want to distance herself from one of the few remaining links she had to her parents.

Niamh shook the thought from her head, grabbed her driver's license off the dresser, and tucked it into the back pocket of her jeans. She spun around on the ball of her boot and eyeballed the room. Even after all these years, she still hadn't grown accustomed to the extravagance surrounding her most days. Di'Lacia, she couldn't wait until she turned eighteen and could leave the house.

She extracted some cash from the top drawer of the antique nightstand beside her bed. Placing the cash in the back pocket of her jeans with her driver's license, she snagged her purple helmet off the back of the door on her way out. She stepped into the hallway—

"Niamh, I was just comin' to see ye," Séamus said.

Shite. She hadn't left fast enough. A good chunk of the time, she usually escaped the house without crossing his path, but some days...there was no avoiding him. She plastered a smile on her mouth and turned around to face him. "I was just on my way to work. What can I do for you?"

"I wanted to ensure ye made time for Briana this weekend. She'll be here to work on your dress."

"Dress?" She tilted her head to the side and pursed her lips. The question had popped out before she could stop it. If she had to be there for a fitting, it could only mean he was demanding her presence at some event he was hosting. This past year she'd been forced to play the part of his date frequently. Talk about a test of control.

"Don't tell me you forgot about my birthday party next weekend."

Sure she had. He was the furthest thing from her mind, unless it included getting away from him. Inwardly, she groaned. She hated dressing up and having to hang on his arm. It was like she was a prized fox he had to show off to his friends. Too bad she couldn't say any of that to him. Instead, she had to pretend she was perfectly okay with it all and simply watch his aura carefully. "Of course not. How could I forget?"

"That's my good girl." He caressed her cheek.

Niamh swallowed the bile that crawled up the back of her throat and her eyebrows pinched together. The sensation of his sausage fingers against her skin grossed her out. Never mind the disturbing idea of being his anything. His intentions had become quite clear over the last few months as the red in his aura intensified each passing day. "I, uh, I need to go. Ye know how, uh, how Rhea hates tardiness."

"Ye know how much I despise you working there, especially with you behind the bar now. All those men...I should send Rooney there to watch over ye." Séamus stroked his chin.

Her eyes widened. Oh, feck no! He already subjected her to living here in this house. She refused to let him take away what little freedom she had. "Ye know Rhea wouldn't tolerate 'em hanging out all evenin'. Plus, I'm capable of takin' care of myself."

Séamus brushed her cheek with the back of his hand. "While I'm sure ye can, I always protect what's mine."

Her nose wrinkled as she tensed and tightened the hold she had on her helmet. *Don't use your powers,* she reminded herself. Yeah, he was a wicked man, but he was still a normal. One she had to get away from now. Slowly, Niamh stepped back. "I have to go."

As she turned away, he grabbed her wrist and squeezed. "Ye just remember who you belong to."

Niamh narrowed her eyes and ground her jaw. There were other places she could go; she didn't have to stay here. Screw her parents' will. Screw the law. It might be the best thing for her if she told him right then she belonged to no man.

Except just past Séamus's shoulder, she glimpsed the one and only reason she stayed: her brother. Quinlan paused outside his bedroom door, glanced in their direction and disappeared down the hallway away from them.

She hadn't figured out yet what was wrong with him. And he was the only thing keeping her here. As soon as she knew what was wrong, she'd get them both out of this awful house. Niamh bit her tongue and returned her attention to Séamus. "I do. Now, I really have to get to work."

"All right, ye can go. We only have another year of this and then we make it all official." He released his hold on her. With a wink, he walked off.

She shuddered at the thought of that man any closer to her than he had been. Not that she'd ever let him get that far. At least she knew his timeframe now. It just meant she had to figure out what was wrong with her brother and get them out of here—soon. Until then, she'd tolerate that disgusting, red-headed tool.

Wiping off the imprint Séamus left on her face, Niamh headed toward the front of the house and left.

# ABOUT THE AUTHOR

**Krys Fenner,** also known as **Brigit Rosé**—like the wine, not the flower—has been infinitely passionate about writing and helping people for as long as she can remember. Having already published nine books, she avidly works on multiple series, from social issues to paranormal romance. While she loves everything she writes, she's genuinely excited about the other series she'll co-authors over the coming year. Krys received an Associate of Arts in Psychology, a Bachelor of Arts in Creative Writing, and is currently working on a Master's degree. When she isn't writing, she's spending time with her three fur babies, Bones, Luna, and Lola. To learn more about Krys Fenner and her upcoming book releases, visit her official website, **https://kbfennerrose.com**.

# UNDER BRIGIT ROSÉ

*Love's Worth Series*
UnHinged
ReIgnited

*Fairytale Retelling Series*
Grace's Beast
*Shakespeare Retelling Series*
Detached

# CO-AUTHORED

*Prisma Isle Series*

Perfectly Reckless
Chaotic Tranquility
Rebel Tides
Siren's Curse
Silencing the Shape Shifter
Insider's Guide
Prisma Isle Coloring & Puzzle Book

# COMING SOON

Inherited (The Guardhian Series)
ReUnited (Love's Worth Series)
Shattered Wonderland (Fairytale Retelling)
Betrayed (Dark Road Series)
Wicked Ground (The Arcarean Academy)
Kingdom of Embers (Prisma Isle Series)